Advance praise for *To the Volcano*

'These assured, accomplished stories are reports from a world in which unacknowledged dark energies undermine and render hollow our bright, rational self-understanding. With passion and intelligence, and rare moral insight, Elleke Boehmer traces the scars left on the psyche by the tortuous histories of the South.'
—J.M. Coetzee

'Compassionate, intelligent and evocative: this is a morally serious writing, lucidly rendered.'　　　　　　　　　—Gail Jones

'Arresting, intriguing, and brilliantly crafted, these stories explore the psychic wounds of our rapidly contracting contemporary world, with its complications of race, migration and trauma. Each unfolds with impeccable pacing, and gradually unveils a deeply humane sense of the world.'　　　　　　　—Kwame Dawes

Praise for Elleke Boehmer

The Shouting in the Dark
Longlisted for the Barry Ronge *Sunday Times* Prize

'The story, as disturbing as it is enthralling, of a girl's struggle to emerge from under the dead weight of her father's oppression while at the same time searching for a secure footing in the moral chaos of South Africa of the apartheid era.'　　　—J. M. Coetzee

'A secret duel to the death between a father and a daughter. Distilled with an intimate sense of history, and very moving, *The Shouting in the Dark* is a powerful novel of memory, family politics and awakening.'　　　　　　　　　　　—Ben Okri

'Boehmer's language is feathery—barely touching the surface of her stories, pregnant with things left unsaid.'
—Zoe Norridge, *Wasafiri*

'An outstanding study of a deeply troubled family against the backdrop of political change, and one girl's resilience in the face of ugly, sharp-edged obstacles.'　　　—Ashley Davies, *The Scotsman*

'As the novel progresses, it becomes clear that this is a double investigation—into the moral chaos of apartheid South Africa as well as self. It is a mark of the writer's skill that this is achieved organically, with nuance, through the telling of Ella's awakening; it never feels heavy-handed or contrived.'

—Melissa de Villiers, *Moving Worlds*

'Like any excellent book it both speaks to the specificity of its historical and geographical location and to the broader nature of human relationships and belonging.'

—Hans Ester, *Nederlands Dagblad*

'This moving story is not to be missed either as a glimpse into the political chaos of Apartheid South Africa or as a beautifully rendered portrait of a childhood deprived of love or comfort. Astounding.'   —The Book Trust

Sharmilla and other portraits

'Elleke Boehmer brings to her stories two qualities that all too often are mutually exclusive: the lucidity of her intelligence and the passion of her engagement.'   —André Brink

'Perceptive new stories.'   —Caryl Phillips

'The accurate simplicity is astonishing, especially because it is present in all her portraits.'   —Tshepo Tshabalala, *Star Tonight*

Nile Baby

'A strange and often unsettling odyssey across England... the novel asks us to consider the complex nature of race and belonging in contemporary Britain.'

—Patrick Flanery, *Times Literary Supplement*

'Boehmer's eye for domestic detail and ear for the nuances of speech whisk the reader in and out of different ways of being... Arnie gradually realizes that life is shaped in unforeseen ways by history.'   —Angela Smith, *The Independent*

'A focused, mesmerizing, and an occasionally stomach-turning story of two twelve-year-olds... [The novel] grasps the enigmatic depths of human, and continental, relations.'   —Derek Attridge

'A moving portrayal of friendship.'

—Mariss Stevens, *NELM News*

Bloodlines
Shortlisted for the Sanlam Prize

'An engrossing and intriguingly told chapter in anti-imperial history.'   —J.M. Coetzee

'A postcolonial fantasia... an imaginative exploration of the possibilities of connectedness... The skilful tracing of bloodlines through several generations makes of a desperate act of violence a token of regeneration.'   —Michiel Heyns, *Sunday Independent*

'A journey into the possible... an extremely good read.'
—*Cape Argus*

'*Bloodlines* is an engaging and compelling book binding a potent theme and memorable characters into a brisk narrative... the writing shows a controlled resonance, the sign of a talent that must not be ignored.'   —*Times Literary Supplement*

An Immaculate Figure

'Remarkable restraint and subtlety.'   —*West Africa*

'A very clever book indeed... It adopts the aesthetic appropriate to a culture in a politically hopeless age.'
—Jenny Turner, *The Guardian*

Screens Against the Sky
Shortlisted for the David Higham Prize

'A brilliant handling of an obsessional mother-daughter relationship... Her descriptions are achingly acute.'   —*Financial Times*

'An astonishing debut... swift, deft and expertly told. With a mordant wit, she shows how discrimination can become as natural as breathing, and as unselfconscious.'
—Penny Perrick, *Sunday Times*

'Eloquently expressive.'   —*The Guardian*

'A beautifully authentic insight into a society turned in on itself in the face of black deprivation.'   —Wendy Woods

'Elegant, percipient writing.'   —Zoe Heller, *The Observer*

TO THE VOLCANO

AND OTHER STORIES

ELLEKE
BOEHMER

First published in 2019 by
Myriad Editions
www.myriadeditions.com

Myriad Editions
An imprint of New Internationalist Publications
The Old Music Hall, 106–108 Cowley Rd, Oxford OX4 1JE

First printing
1 3 5 7 9 10 8 6 4 2

'Evelina' was first published in *Mascara Literary
Review* 23 (March 2019)

Every effort has been made to obtain the necessary
permissions for use of copyright material quoted. If there have
been any omissions, we apologise and shall be pleased to make
appropriate acknowledgement in any future edition.

A CIP catalogue record for this book
is available from the British Library

ISBN (pbk) 978-1-912408-24-5
ISBN (ebk) 978-1-912408-25-2

Designed and typeset in Palatino
by New Internationalist, Oxford

Printed and bound in Great Britain
by Clays Ltd, Elcograf S.p.A.

For SM

If you keep going south you will meet yourself.
Kudzanai-Violet Hwami

I shall make for the south...and never go north again.
Katherine Mansfield, last letter to Ida Baker (unsent), Fontainebleau, France.

Contents

Contents

The Child in the Photograph

'*FROM AFRICA* IS HOW they introduce me,' Luanda tells her mother on her first trunk-call home. 'Isn't it funny, Ma? Just *from Africa*. Can you believe…?'

A crackle zaps her mother's reply.

After the Angolan port-city, Luanda tells her fellow Masters students in Development. Yes, that's my name. But Angola's not my country. See if you can guess my country. For starters, it's landlocked and dry and farther south than the Sahara. Getting warmer? Luanda laughs. My country also has diamonds. That's a dead giveaway. What d'you call yourselves, *Development* students? My country has loads of diamonds.

'You tell them,' her mother says down a suddenly clear phone line. 'Your country's brightest diamond. Easily. Brighter than any star.'

Luanda shuts her eyes. Her mother's voice is as close as if she were right here beside her in the college phone booth. She pictures her there in the living-room at home, her big thighs spread across the fake-leather easy-chair beside the TV. She sees the black plastic mouthpiece wedged between her cheek and her shoulder in that clever way of hers, like the PA she is. She sees her red-painted fingernails twisting around the black telephone cord.

On the wall across from her mother are her own framed certificates. Luanda pictures them clearly: the certificates arranged on the wall in two columns, her university medals and honours and essay prizes, the rungs of the long ladder she has climbed to get to this ancient stone college with its single shabby telephone booth and muddy McDonald's wrappings thick on the floor. She sees the gold-embossed lettering on the certificates catch the horizontal light of the setting sun.

'Nothing short of a fancy sundial,' her mother's boyfriend Pa once mock-scolded. 'Look, the letters even cast a shadow.'

'Proud of her,' her mother staunchly said.

A pink-and-white hand beats against the glass of the phone-booth door. The glass is cloudy with condensation. Luanda can't see the body behind the hand.

'Can hardly believe it, being here,' she yells over another squall of static. 'The other students can't believe it either. I mean, *me* being *here*. When I walk into a room, they stop talking, they all stare.'

'So you're educating them. No matter how ancient and clever, they have something to learn.'

Luanda laughs at her mother's joke, if it was a joke. She laughs the open-mouthed cawing laugh that she shares with her mother. *Ha-ha-ha* it goes, rasping to a close. Some days even Nana can't tell their laughs apart.

'I must go, Ma.'

'Next time Nana will come say hello. Sorry, Lu. She was here but she's run off.'

The swallow Luanda now makes hurts her chest. The hand again slaps the door.

Her mother is calling bye, over and over again. Bye, Luanda echoes her, bye. Then she presses the silver *Next Call* button and her mother's voice cuts out. She stands holding the receiver in her hand, the dial-tone purring.

She rubs the condensation on the glass with her sleeve. Whoever was out there has given up. The foyer is empty. She scrapes off the McDonald's wrapping sticking to her shoe and takes the stairs up to her room two at a time, breathing hard with relief, almost laughing, as if she has escaped something, has got through an obstacle course without injury.

Luanda relies on her laugh in the days ahead, at the hundred ice-breaker parties and inductions she lists in beautiful schoolgirl cursive in her diary. She laughs and watches her laugh's effect on people, how it makes them turn towards her and smile. Laughing, she slides across thickly carpeted rooms between shuffling clusters of guests like a rain droplet down a windscreen, laughing when they stumble on her name, laughing when they ask about her course and then forget and ask again, laughing, laughing, till the other students start calling her Laughing Luanda. Laughing, she asks them to stop.

She wanders around the old university town, *her* university town, believe it or not, but now she doesn't laugh. A dream is beyond laughter and all this is beyond even a dream, it's beyond her imagination. Not in a thousand years could she have dreamed up this perfect green grass in the quadrangles or the spreading trees like pictures or the all-surrounding stone: the stone walls, stone flags, the Gothic stone arch of her bedroom window looking like it was stamped out with a cookie cutter, the stone steps up to her room worn away by the numberless footsteps of numberless students. 'I mean, *stone*, Ma, *cut* stone, *worn* stone, like it's melting,' she said on the phone and still couldn't quite believe it. She could not have dreamed up the pure coldness that rises from the stone and instantly chills her hand when she touches it. That anything could be so cold! She could not have imagined the cold dark shadows that wait in the corners of the stone and never shift. Even at noon they don't shrink away.

Her university before this one, where she received the trophies and certificates on her mother's wall, is no more than a cluster of single-storey prefab blocks built on the surrounding red sand. On the side of each building a single huge air-conditioning unit sticks out like an ear-stud. The dusty area in front of the admin buildings is called the English garden though the only plants that grow there are cactuses. The English garden! Looking around at the green grass, the spreading oaks, Luanda wants to laugh, remembering, but catches herself in time and feels ashamed.

She takes pictures of her stone window arch with the Polaroid camera her family gave her at the airport—Ma, Pa, Gogo, Nana, everyone. She photographs her window first from the inside, from several angles, then from the street, looking up. These are the first photographs she takes here at her new university.

She sends the photos home folded inside a long letter about the ancient stone and her new classmates, their difficult-to-understand English, the day-in day-out black clothing that they wear like a uniform. She tells them that the only place to get her hair done is out of town, two bus rides away, close to the industrial area. She writes about the café the students all visit after class, Luigi's, how everyone helps her with her coffee order, each shouting louder than the last. Latte, macchiato, espresso, some of the new words for coffee she has never seen let alone said before. Up to now she had only ever tasted Ricoffy Instant. She tells them about her dissertation topic. The question of whether the water that flows over your land belongs to you. Especially when that land is dry. The whole thing sounds funny over here where it rains every day.

Should she be *more* amazed? she asks them all in closing. Her way is to think about the future and the next generation, not the past. But these walls and pillars and the solid stuff inside the walls—the paintings, great oak tables, massive card catalogues—these things have stood here just like they do today for hundreds of years. They will also go on standing just like they do for more hundreds of years.

Do you see what I'm saying, Ma, Pa, Gogo? They were the future then and somehow, though they are so old, they are still the future now.

On top of the bookcase in her bedroom with its cold stone walls she places two framed photographs. Ma and her Tata on their wedding day: Ma in a ridiculous short tulle veil, Tata already bowed and sick. And a studio portrait, herself in her graduation gear at the university with the cactuses. Into a corner of the wedding photograph she wedges a passport-sized photograph of a laughing toothless child in a red dress.

'My little sister, Nana,' Luanda tells her Development classmates when they come to her room to drink tea. She goes to their bedrooms to drink tea also. Sometimes she says more. 'My little sister, Nana, trying to grow some teeth,' she tells Archie, an angular English boy who did *something in Africa* on his gap year. 'See, we have milk teeth in Africa too.'

Then, laughing, she changes the subject. 'Now, seriously, how do you manage to cope with the cold in this country? Is it M and S underwear?' And she laughs again.

She attends a gala party to mark the college's eight-hundredth birthday. She stands beside the grand piano in the corner, champagne flute in hand. Can you believe it, *that* many centuries old? she imagines telling her mother on the phone.

This time people for some reason come over to her. A college fellow touches his champagne flute to hers and asks how Development is going. Laughter bursts from her mouth, she can't help it. She grips the skinny forearm of his wife standing beside him and, without spilling her glass, whispers into her clip-on earring, 'Yes, I'd prefer a cup of tea, too.'

The College President invites Luanda to High Table. She wears a blue-and-white waxed cotton dress that Ma's dressmaker made. The cold falls from the stone walls in slabs and lies against her skin. She wishes she had brought a woollen scarf, a shawl, a blanket. Opposite, the President's wife sits with a billowing cream bow at her throat looking like the Prime Minister herself.

A Very Big Man once in Government, our College President, she begins a fresh letter to her family. We ate a five-course meal on a stage and I sat beside him. I helped him with his wine glass because his hands shake. His wife motioned me using just her chin.

But Luanda doesn't write about the dinners in London that follow. There are too many—the dinners with the College President and his wife and people they call the Great and the Good in huge hotels with heavy glass doors that bellhops in uniform open silently as they approach. Luanda sweeps in between the two of them, the President and his wife, taller than them both, even without her head-wrap. Under her waxed cotton dresses she wears polo-neck jumpers and nylon spencers, sometimes even long-johns, like on freezing July nights at home.

'Never knew any country could have enough Big people to produce a whole group called Great and Good,' she tells her fellow guests over canapés and wonders why they laugh, including the College President. Which bit of what she said was funny?

She doesn't write that some evenings she goes to London with just the College President. Lady Sarah tires easily, he says. The trip to London is too tiring for her. You can help him with his wine glass, Lady Sarah says.

Luanda also doesn't write that one afternoon in the first-class railway carriage on the way back from London the College President asked to touch her hair. She doesn't write that she let him, which is to say, she didn't want to say no, she didn't like to. She doesn't write that, when he touched her hair, he called her Africa's diamond—like her mother, but differently, too.

She doesn't write that the very next day she paid the College President's wife a visit. It was the middle of the afternoon so Lady Sarah made Earl Grey tea and they ate the shortbread biscuits that she had brought along.

Drinking tea that afternoon, Luanda tells Lady Sarah about the English garden full of cactuses at her old university. She describes the dressmaker's tiny shop in the main street of their middle-sized town, which is in fact the country's capital. This is the shop where the waxed cotton dresses that Lady Sarah has said she likes are made and also the fancy head-wraps in matching cottons for people who enjoy making a bold entrance 'like you know I do'.

'I want to order a couple more head-wraps from home,' Luanda says, finishing her biscuit and putting her hand against the side of her head. 'I like to wear my hair uncovered like this, natural, but lately I've had second thoughts. Maybe I should get a weave or some braids. The thing is, you wouldn't believe how the Great and the Good like to touch my hair, Lady Sarah. You wouldn't believe how many. They lean across and give it a feel, a pinch, you know, how people do with pregnant ladies, making free with their stomachs.'

The President's wife suddenly blushes, and Luanda looks out of the window. She looks out of the window a long time.

She wants Lady Sarah to reassure herself that she, Luanda, has not seen her blush.

~

By November Luanda is exhausted. 'Whacked out', she tells the College porters, laughing. 'You guys taught me the word. I'm just whacked out. Development is tough work.'

She presents a paper to the Masters class on the insensitivity of inequality coefficients as a measure of water scarcity in African countries with low annual rainfall. It's tiring just to outline the topic. She stays up all night to finish the thing and discovers how long the winter darkness really lasts.

At the end of the presentation, her classmates clap and her tutor smiles. He asks her to give him a copy of the paper. There are one or two aspects he'd like to reflect upon further.

'Never thought about it enough, Luanda,' her friend Archie says. 'The equations don't pick up on a basic need like water. Also, I wanted to ask, were you maybe thinking of coming along to the pub this evening? We've missed you lately.'

She nods yes, but doesn't show up.

'Fell asleep over my pot noodle,' she tells Archie in class the next day.

She also misses the President's All Saints party. *I'm so sorry*, she writes on the embossed college notepaper the porters sell her, 5p a page, her pen sinking into the thick paper like a foot into a mattress. *I fell asleep in the library. I won't let it happen again.*

'Your family called,' George the porter on duty tells her. 'Yes, all the way from Africa. They asked you to call them. They say they haven't had a letter in ages.'

'But I don't have enough pound coins saved up right now to call Africa,' Luanda says, laughing a little. 'Plus the letter I've written is so fat it'll take a fortune to send.'

Archie comes over to her room for a visit. He finds her sitting up against the side of her bed in a plush pink dressing gown apparently doing nothing.

'Mind if I come in, Lu?' he says, pushing open the door. 'I've brought some brandy. Duty-free, Nairobi airport. It'll make a nice nightcap.'

'Hardly as though I need help with sleeping, Archie,' Luanda says, yawning energetically. She waves at the kettle on the window sill. 'You go ahead.'

He switches on the kettle, puts a teabag in a mug, adds brandy. He is missing something—yes, that's it, the laugh that follows most of what she says.

He comes to sit beside her on the floor, his back against the mattress, the mug of hot tea and brandy between his feet.

'So what're you up to tonight, Lu?'

'Not much. Just sitting and thinking, you know, thinking and not thinking…'

'Penny for them, as we say?'

She lays her arm on the edge of the bed and props her head on her arm.

'Not sure I can put it into words, Archie. It's late and I'm sleepy. I'm incredibly sleepy.'

Archie looks round the room so like his own, the fatty Blu Tack marks on the walls, the desk and lamp and bookcase, the row of library books, the cards and photographs on the top shelf of the bookcase.

'Lu, there's something different, you've changed your photographs.'

She raises her head for a second, pillows her cheek back on her arm. Her Omega alarm-clock ticks in its propped-open case on the floor beside the bed.

'The other day I was tidying,' she eventually says. 'I tidied all the invitations away and I put the little photograph back in my travel album. It was unframed. I didn't want it to get spoiled.'

'The one of your sister.'

'Yes, Nana. My sister.'

Archie edges a little closer, close enough for his shoulder to touch the tips of her fingers. He swallows the last of his tea-and-brandy. Her eyes are suddenly fixed on him.

'You could let me hold you a bit, Lu,' he says and moves closer again. 'As you're so tired. We could lie on the bed and I could just hold you, if you didn't mind. I could tell you about the summer I planted trees in the Highlands. How close the sky looked.'

He waits.

'Lu,' he whispers and puts his hand lightly against her cheek. 'If you'd let me, I'd like to get to know you better. I'd like to very much.'

The free hand lying in her lap comes up quite suddenly and pushes his hand away.

He shuffles back and, when she still says nothing, gets up awkwardly. His left leg has gone to sleep.

'Sorry, Lu, sorry, I didn't mean... I'm really sorry. Look, you know I like to see you. You know I'm always happy to see you.'

'Archie, please just get out.' Her voice is back in the room. Moisture shines in the grooves beneath her lower eyelids.

'Don't come in like that again,' she says as he pulls the door open. 'My unlocked door isn't an invitation. I leave it unlocked so I don't feel boxed in. *Sealed in a stone-cold tomb*—remember the Christmas carol.' She almost laughs.

~

Luanda now comes to classes late. She slips into the seats at the back and spends her time cross-hatching shapes in her notebook. To Archie she says hello just the same as before.

Then she's not in class at all.

Lu must be in the library, the others say, she's a great one for working round the clock. Archie remembers the thing she said about the Christmas carol and checks the library. She's not there.

Perhaps she uses another library, the others say. Ask someone in her college, the porters are her friends. And Christmas is coming. Luanda is surely joining in somewhere, getting her essays in early. Didn't she say she'd try to make it over to Europe—Switzerland, she said? Didn't she want to see some snow?

After dinner, Archie takes a walk past her college. He checks her window. The light is on. There are shadows moving across the ceiling.

The next day he sees the books that were in her bedroom the night he visited on the book-returns trolley in the library. He takes them out himself, leafs through each one. There might be a note, something to tell him what's up. He finds an old train ticket dated from before the summer, before Lu ever arrived in England.

On the final Monday of term, a frosty day, he writes her a Christmas card, a plain seasonal greeting, English as it comes. He puts her name at the top and *Archie* at the bottom. Then he scrawls, *Look forward to seeing you back next term.*

The line is barely legible so she can easily ignore it.

Should he have said *back*? he asks himself, sliding the card into the envelope. He could better have left it out.

He walks the card round to her college. The porter watches him slide it into her mailbox.

'No telling when she'll pick that up,' the porter says darkly. 'In and out of here at all hours, she is.'

Archie sees the business card tucked into the metal name bracket below the mailbox.

Kids' Hair Workshop, the card says. *Weaves, Cornrows, Braids. Face-painting While-U-Wait. Horshill Community Centre. Once a week only. Don't miss out!*

'She's off to Switzerland, I think? She wanted to see some snow.'

'Like I said, there's no telling with Lu. No telling what's up from one minute to the next. Doing stuff with kids. Collecting toys to send to Africa. It's all for development, she says.'

'Yes,' Archie says, feeling suddenly tired. 'We're all studying Development as hard as we can.'

Luanda's reply to his card arrives at his college within hours, a Christmas card showing a red robin standing on a patch of blue snow. There is nothing written on either side of the gold *Merry Christmas.* On the facing page are two scrawled lines.

I've found a park outside of town. It has a duck pond, a putting range, the works. Let's do a Christmas outing. Tomorrow 2pm.

~

They meet at the bus-stop beside the coffee shop in a dense drizzle. Luanda presents her cheek for a kiss and Archie presses his lips to her skin. She is icy cold. Silver droplets shine like glitter in her hair.

Their bus passes ten or more stops. Then Luanda clears a round hole in the fogged-up window and elbows him.

She leads him down a long suburban street, past a small roundabout, into a narrower street. The drizzle has faded away. They reach a green metal boom and a grassy car-park, a shuttered ice-cream hut.

'See,' Luanda says with satisfaction as they walk past the hut. 'Park all around, far as your eyes can see, park, park and more park, flat as flat. Flat, straight avenue, big flat duck pond.

Not a single piece of old stone in sight.'

Archie follows her along a muddy path beyond the putting green to the pond.

A squashed fruit-juice carton floats on the surface of the pond amongst the dead leaves and some crumpled sheets of paper. The paper is silver Christmas wrap. A straw is stuck in the carton like an antenna. There are no ducks to be seen. They sit down at opposite ends of the metal bench.

'I come here quite often,' Luanda says after a bit. 'The first time, there was a granny with a toddler. They were feeding the ducks bread, sliced bread, I remember. *Developed* bread.' She begins to laugh, then coughs. 'There were a lot of ducks here that day, brown ducks. I looked at the ducks, the toddler and the gran. I looked and looked and then I cried, I couldn't help it.'

'You cried?'

'Yes, I cried, but not that they'd notice. See, it was so beautiful, so peaceful, the pond, the ducks. I thought how much I'd like to take Nana to this park. This would be the first duck pond she'd ever seen. It's the first duck pond I've ever seen. At home, we have a park in town, but it's sandy. There's no grass. There's a meerkat enclosure and beside it a vendor sells samosas from an ice-cream cart. There's a shade cover over the viewing area that the Australian embassy donated. We sometimes take Nana there. We like to watch the meerkats. People feed them samosas though they shouldn't.'

She folds her arms tight across her chest. Her breathing is odd, as if she's swallowing hiccups.

'I've been mistaken, Archie,' she suddenly blurts. 'I thought I could start a life here, away from them all, on my own. I thought I could fulfil my dream, study Development where everyone said Development began. I thought I could, but...'

'But...?' says Archie.

'But,' says Luanda. 'But.'

The light begins to fade. They walk back to the green boom, the shuttered ice-cream hut.

'You go on ahead,' Luanda leans against the side of hut. 'I'll stay here a bit longer. I'll make my own way back.'

She holds out her hand. Her grip is fierce. She holds Archie's hand for a long time before she steps away.

~

The college tonight is quiet. In the front quad the Christmas tree is a tall dark spire. The porters have forgotten to switch on its lights.

Luanda's room is filled with a soft golden glow. She has turned off the overhead bulb and thrown a scarf over her desk lamp. She pulls two sheets of embossed college notepaper from her desk drawer.

Dear Archie, she writes in her beautiful cursive, *I'm sorry not to say goodbye in person. I love so much about being here and even about Development (ha-ha) but I have decided to suspend my studies. I miss my family too much and I don't want to carry on, at least for now.*

To the President's wife she writes the same message, minus the *(ha-ha).*

Then she continues, *I miss Nana especially. I think it is too much for my mother to look after her on her own. Ma has already raised her kids and Nana is not her job to look after. She's my job, my daughter. I wanted to let you know. As she gets older I will try to make it up to everyone. Most of all, I will try to make it up to her.*

She reads through both letters and adds *Happy New Year!* to the end of each, then slides the sheets of notepaper into their matching embossed envelopes.

~

At the end of spring term Archie and the other Development students have coffee in Luigi's café off the High Street. They have kept on coming since the beginning of the course. These days Luigi gives them double espressos for the price of a single.

They sit at their table in the corner under the noticeboard where customers pin up their business cards. Luigi insists that every customer leaves a card. Everyone has something to sell, he says, even you students. Maybe you do typing, maybe you do haircutting. Whatever you do, make a card, let the world know.

'Sitting here I can't help thinking about Lu,' Archie says. 'Remember Luanda? How she learned to say all the words for coffee.' He notices how good it feels to say her name. 'She virtually lived in here some days.'

'Did she ever send news?' someone asks.

'No, she didn't,' Archie says.

He is looking at the noticeboard at the same moment that he speaks. It is like a conjuring trick. It is as if her name calls up something, as if the writing on the noticeboard makes him see what he might otherwise have missed. As he speaks he reads the half-familiar words on the business card. *Kids' Hair Workshop.* He knows he has read that card somewhere before.

Now he notices the Polaroid photo stuck directly beneath the business card. The Polaroid colours are fresh and bright. In the photo a young woman in a cotton print dress is holding hands with a child in a smaller version of the same dress. It is unmistakeably Luanda. Luanda and the child are both wearing cross-braids. They point at each other's cross-braids. They are both laughing. The child's front teeth are growing in.

Weaves, Cornrows, Braids, Archie reads again. *Don't miss out!*

Luigi puts down their espressos and follows the line of Archie's stare.

'Arrived last week,' he says. 'Our Luanda, she keeps in touch. How we miss her. But I'm so happy she is happy. Isn't it good to see her laughing again at last?'

South, North

i. *left from the metro stop, skip three streets, and then left again*
Centre Pompidou. Tuileries. Louvre. Arc de Triomphe. Lise
walks her fingers from name to sacred name on the map spread
on her thigh.

At each metro stop she glances up quickly to check the
station, then looks straight back down at her lap. There are
people standing up in the carriage but she avoids making eye
contact. The world doesn't need to see how excited she is. She
knows how she gets when she's excited, the raw wonder gaping
from her eyes like a kid's at Christmas.

The Seine, yes, the Seine, she walks her fingers. Île-de-
France, Notre Dame, she cups her hand over the heart of the
map, more history and more energy crowded into this inch than
a hundred inches of the map back home. It's Paris, really Paris,

here, all around, in every direction, as she comes up now from the metro, no, *le métro,* and sees the evening sky pouring pink over the Place de la Concorde.

Her first destination is the youth hostel off the Rue de Rivoli. She sounds out Rue de Rivoli under her breath, in the back of her throat, Frenching the Rs. Stupid to say, but it's hard to believe that this crowd she's moving through speaks *French,* all these people speak and think in French. If she opens her mouth and says Rue de Rivoli, they'll listen and understand her, these words that she has spent the past couple of years learning to say with no one but her maths teacher to check whether she's making sense or not.

For now, though, she doesn't open her mouth to speak. Months ago, in her far-distant desert town in her far-distant country, she picked out this street and this street number on the map. She made a cross in light pencil on the spot and wrote herself directions in her notebook, this notebook open here in her hand.

left from the metro stop, skip three streets, and then left again.

Backpackers her age sit in the neon-lit youth-hostel common room drinking hot chocolate with rum and talking about other places they have visited—Morocco, Sicily, Istanbul, even India. They exchange tips for cadging rides in Turkey and ferry trips in the Balearics and finding cheap meals everywhere.

Someone talks about hitchhiking in the Algarve and getting picked up by a bra salesman. Three times the girl repeats the punchline. 'So I asked to put my backpack in the boot, and, oh my god, it was nothing but a mass of under-wiring and padded cups!'

Lise does not join the group. She has no travel stories to share. She has visited no other places. Her shoulders are sore from carrying her backpack because it's stuffed full of her complete library of French books, ten of them. She gets into her top bunk, puts her head on the thin hostel pillow and faces the wall. It'll be morning in less than a minute, she tells herself.

ii. *right and right again and...north*

In the grey morning light Lise dresses quietly, jeans, jumper, boots. She bundles her hair into a ponytail, out of the way. No one else in the dorm is awake. The person in the bunk-bed below is snoring throatily, her face pressed into her pillow. Lise eats the polished green apple she bought yesterday at a metro kiosk. She nibbles and slides her mouth over the fruit so as not to make noise.

She squats down to prepare her daypack. How many times, back home, at the airport, over and over, has she gone through this routine? She closes her eyes and takes from her big backpack a blind sampling of four books. Each book is wrapped in a clear plastic sleeve. She opens her eyes and, fine, yes, she approves the selection—two Zolas, one in translation, *L'Assommoir*, that's good, also *Nana*.

The books bristle with post-it notes but she won't look at the marked pages now. When her favourite passages point to things here, now, close by, within reach, unbelievable, out here in the streets of Paris, and she is in Paris and must go find them.

She squares up the books and slides them into her daypack, wedging the pile into place with her disposable plastic rain jacket and a bottle of water she refilled last night in the hostel bathroom. She squeezes in a packet of madeleines, her first madeleines ever, also from the metro kiosk, but she won't open them yet because the plastic wrapping is too crackly. The fold-out map of Paris she puts in her pocket, opened to the right section. Keep it nice. The map is on loan from her maths teacher.

He not only knows French, he's also the only person from home who has visited Paris. That is, till now, till this visit.

She folds the big backpack flap over the remaining books, pulls the drawstring tight and hefts the bag onto her bunk. Wait there till later—she pats the area of its shoulders as if it were a person.

If she could, she'd take along the whole pack of books. With these second-hand books in their plastic sleeves, she has taught herself French. Every evening on the formica-top table in the kitchen at home she spread out the English translations side by side with the French originals. She read back and forth, from the French to the English and back again, Zola especially, but also Balzac, Hugo, Dumas. She listened to the heat crackling the corrugated roof and the dry wind stripping bark off the eucalyptus tree beside the house and rattling it down on the metal overhead, and she read.

'And this is why your father drives a fork-lift and I clear tables?' her mother grumbled as she wiped the floor around her feet. 'For you to sit and learn a language no one around here even speaks?'

Lise said nothing back. She had no answer to this question. Once she said that reading these books had changed her world but she saw her mother wince and knew it was unfair and also untrue, because her world hadn't yet changed—at least not then.

She tries not to remember the thing her mother said in reply, pushing the damp cloth around the table legs.

'What's so bad about this world then, that you want to change it? My parents sweated blood to get out to this country, make a new life.'

Lise lets herself out of the hostel by pressing the green buzzer. The morning smells damp and fresh. A cleaner is sloshing sudsy water onto the pavement and sweeping it away with a broom.

She sidesteps the water, turns right and right again and sets off, heading north, her refolded map snug in her pocket.

No aim, that is her aim, no special destination, other than to find Zola's streets, because she read him first and liked him from the start. She wants to say she liked him best but at the time obviously she couldn't. Now she can say she likes him best because she has read the others.

Zola writes a film. She can imagine everything he describes, the things, the doings, the people. Reading him she can feel the pink heat in Gervaise's laundry when it's snowing outside. She can imagine Goujet's forge shaking as he beats out a perfect bolt. She can see him pounding his mighty passion into its precise and perfect edges.

Zola's world is as full and cluttered and heavy with things as her own desert world back home is empty, kind of, in the opposite direction.

Reading at the formica kitchen table under the crackling roof, she began to mark up her map and plan this long journey. She wanted to walk in Gervaise's footsteps as she delivered pressed collars to the doors of her favourite clients. She wanted to trace the route past the chain-makers, cobblers, fishmongers, watchmakers, dye-shops and milliners that Gervaise took every day, peering into their fogged-up windows. The name of every one of those shops—milliners, dye-shops, etcetera—she, Lise, can say in French.

She raised money for the trip by selling her bike and the sewing machine she got for her fourteenth birthday. Six nights a week she worked the late shift at the drive-thru fast-food servo beside the petrol station on the edge of town, the joint where the truckers and the rest of the inter-state traffic stop. She bought French books in the second-hand shop and she learned more French. She studied her maths teacher's map.

Some nights when the air-conditioning was on too high

and the servo was freezing, she took her books outside and read them under the neon of the street lights. Here she could see the road trains coming from miles away, the road through town running south, north like a line of longitude with barely a kink in it.

'My suggestion,' said her maths teacher, stroking his tortoiseshell cat that late afternoon she went to say goodbye, 'Go north of the Sacré-Cœur, just walk. See what you can see.'

See what you can see, she tells herself now, turning into a narrow street, yellow refuse bags in a pile beside a shuttered restaurant, still heading north, slightly west. This route should take her to the next big avenue. The marks on her map point beyond Montmartre, beyond the Gare du Nord, and then further again.

Zola's Goutte d'Or—it will be there somewhere, she knows, buried in the underlying pattern of the streets, sifted into the cracks between the paving stones and the joins between the buildings. It will be there in the shape of the apartment blocks, how they cut up the sky, and in the arch of the doorways leading into dark courtyards with spiral staircases in the corners, the same corners where Nana practised doing the splits in her dishevelled dress.

The street or perhaps boulevard she is on is long, it's more like several streets strung together. Intersection follows intersection and pavement follows pavement. Clouds creep in over the sun, and flashes of pale light pass over the slate-blue roofs and the high-up windows.

The rain holds off but it is past two before she gets to the Sacré-Cœur area. There will be almost as much distance again to go. Standing in a doorway, she checks her map and drinks some water. She slides two madeleines out of the crackly plastic wrapping, tries one. It tastes of almost nothing, grease and sweetness. She throws it away and folds a corner of the wrapping around the other one. When she lifts her pack back on she feels the reassuring drag of her books across her shoulder blades.

iii. *south...north...*

At four o'clock she decides, this is it, close to it, this long narrow street with its far distances now veiled in a light drizzle, the light disappearing. This has to be it. She looks up, left, right. On both sides are enormous concrete apartment blocks stained with the rain. There are no cafés any more, no smell of coffee. There is a slick but ashy feel to the pavements, as if the drizzle had turned granular.

See what you can see, she tells herself again. Don't expect a thing.

Behind one of these dreary facades, four or five flights up, Gervaise once took her bright tongs and expertly goffered a lace shirt.

Lise turns left down another long street, then left again. She pauses on a corner to put on her raincoat. There are more pedestrians than before—shoppers, perhaps, or commuters, hurrying past head-down in the thickening grey light. She passes key-cutting kiosks, betting shops, tiny convenience stores, KFCs. Many shopfronts are boarded up. The shutters are graffitied in lettering she can't read. In the darkened doorways huddle human-shaped piles of rags.

Would Gervaise have hurried past these people without a word, Lise wonders, as she is doing now?

She thinks she sees a street sign, Rue des Poissonniers. That really could be it, an axis point, but the drizzle in her eyes makes her blink and squint and the crowd shifts her along. Her collapsed bun is a piece of dank animal on her neck. When she again looks up, she can't find the sign.

By now her boots are letting in the wet. The boots have no

tread and slip-slide across the paving stones. At home it barely ever rains.

She slips into a dollar-stretcher kind of shop, its entrance cheerful with hanging plastic flags. Imagine that. She travelled thousands of miles to get here and takes shelter in the same kind of shop you'd find in the small mall at home.

She can see the small mall now, the shops in their line— the dollar-stretcher, the card and gift shop, the shoe shop, the chemist, and then at the end the post office. At Christmas the flower-bed in front of the post office is hazy-blue with agapanthus.

She is so far from anywhere familiar she forgives herself this dollar-stretcher.

She walks amongst display units piled full of multipack clothes in basic colours, white cotton vests, navy and black tops and leotards, all exactly the same as you get at home. Her raincoat is dripping in her wake. Should she take it off? She checks around to see who has noticed.

She is aware of the man minutes before she actually sees him, lays her eyes on him. *Laying eyes on* is what her mother says. To Lise it sounds vaguely disgusting. She anyway doesn't want to lay eyes on this person. Already he is drawing in close, a thin figure, tall, very tall in fact, murmuring something, moving clockwise around this display unit full of peaked caps machine-embroidered with the names of American baseball teams. *Yankees. Red Sox. Angels.*

Ff, ff, he seems to be spluttering, hurrying to get the words out. She sees he is as soaked as she is, his shoulders blotched dark with damp.

She walks deeper into the store, beyond the hosiery, beyond the dishcloths and handtowels. The figure, the man, walks faster, too. She sidesteps, circles around a square counter. White cotton socks are on sale, lying in piles, a pack of five for two euros.

He is on the opposite side and she can't help it, she lays her eyes on him, she looks him full in the face. She shouldn't have done this. His eye sockets are deep and shadowy and his eyes stare.

A jab of fear goes through her and then a strange jab of longing. For some reason she thinks of diesel, the smell of fuel, engines grinding. She thinks of the big road-trains shifting gear as they heave through her desert town at night, thundering past the drive-thru fast-food, bulleting on south or north through the desert.

She thinks of the tired blue-black eyes of the truckers when they come in for a burger, and the rustling and rattling of the dry wind in the big River Reds when there are no trucks. She thinks of the one traffic light on Main Street shifting green to yellow to red to green, sometimes without a single car passing, even in the daytime.

The man is talking at her. *Ff, ff,* he says, and then other sounds, with a catch in the throat, but she doesn't follow them—she doesn't want to follow.

She can tell he is talking at her, though, because his eyes reach for hers, they lay themselves on her, they insist she looks back. If she moves right he moves left so he is still opposite, still looking at her. She tries to stare to the side of his head but this makes his voice increase in volume. She moves again, and he moves, like in hide-and-seek. She pauses and he pauses, as if she was his reflection, he was her mirror.

His tongue flickers between his teeth like a lizard's. *Ff, ff.* Suddenly it's hard to breathe.

Then he stops dodging. He darts around the unit, fast, but she is as quick as he is.

The security guard is standing to the left of the shop entrance, looking out at the rain. His uniform is black with a silver leopard logo on his breast pocket. She rushes at him, brakes just in front of his feet. She sees he has a small dark beard and dark liquid-brown eyes. Her mother would say *soulful*—soulful eyes.

To her left she is aware of the tall figure moving out into the street, still talking, *ff ff ff*. He does not look up. She sees for the first time his stoop, his shoulders hunched inside his wet denim jacket, the thick dark hair curling over the collar. The side of his face as he glances up then down the street is flushed and his neck corded, the skin pulled tight, liverish. It shocks her to see this. Seeing his colour, hearing him talk, she knows he will wait for her. Somewhere outside, he will be waiting.

'Help me, please, *s'il vous plaît*, I need help,' is the first thing she tells the security guard, mostly in English, then when he looks at her hard in French.

He points across the road, but where? She peers. He shrugs and sets out with her. Her feet in their slippery soles slide over the paving stones. They walk three shops down, then across at the lights, and three shops up again. He points to a place where the road surface shines with wetness and lightly touches her elbow.

'Don't slip,' she hears him say, in French. After a pause he adds, in English, 'Those unhealthy demons, they're so heavily awake.'

But she must have imagined this. She thought he didn't speak English. Or maybe he spoke in French. She's got so good it was *as if* it were English.

Still touching her elbow the security guard steers her into a yellow space, a teleshop, and everything is suddenly warm, dry, calm. The walls are lined in glass-fronted wooden phone booths, ten or twelve. The counter here on the left is stacked high with shiny tin cans of olive oil. On the yellow-gloss panel behind the counter hang bright framed posters of football teams. Relief goes through her in a wave.

iv. *neither left nor right*

'A drink to go with your call?' the elderly proprietor behind the teleshop counter says in English. With his triangular white beard he points to a tall fridge in the corner.

Lise shakes her head, goes into the second booth. In the first booth the caller is saying 'si' and then 'si' quietly, at intervals. In her booth is a shelf, a dial phone attached to the wall, a stool. A dark circle halos the door handle.

She rubs her damp hands together to get them dry. Her breathing stays fast and uneven. She tries closing her mouth and taking big breaths through her nose.

She reads the instructions for making long-distance calls and dials the home phone number. As she dials she counts the hours on her fingers, then puts down the receiver. Way too early, thoughtless to disturb them this early.

She waits. It is warm and cosy in the booth. She reads the signage again. French is so much easier to understand printed black-on-white. She fingers the books in the sodden bag on her lap, their corners still pointy, firm. Why she wrapped them in plastic back before she left home. She looks at the bits of themselves other people have left in here, the greasy finger marks on the phone, the initials scribbled on the wooden walls in biro, the whorl of dirt around the door handle. She dials once more. The phone rings. After a while the ring cuts out.

It seems like she got the time wrong. They must have already left for work.

She sees her mother standing at the washing line in her bra and knickers, that soft freckled skin on her stomach. On hot summer mornings her mother does her chores before she puts on her brown-check uniform, to keep it fresh. Though when she, Lise, is home, hanging out the laundry is usually her job.

She thinks of the clothes drying fast and stiff on the clothes line and under the line the patch of artificial grass Dad put in last summer when there was no rain at all. In the early morning the grassy patch is cool to stand on. She thinks it would be nice if the teleshop served hot coffee as well as cold drinks.

She imagines her mother's voice saying hello and then her name, two syllables, Li-se, not one, as they do here.

'You *would* go,' she hears her mother saying. 'So what's the point of phoning now, when you're halfway across the world?'

The receiver is buzzing in her hand. Lise returns it to the bracket and sits for a while longer, holding her backpack in her lap, feeling the weight of her books. She held her books in her lap exactly like this all those nights in the servo out on the highway, reading without letting the manager see. On slow nights, though, he turned a blind eye. There were so many nights when no trucks stopped and the burger fat congealed on the grill in the kitchen.

She remembers the last heatwave they had, when she stood in the middle of the highway in the darkness, one foot on either side of the white line, the ice-blue evening light floating over the southern horizon like a spaceship. The warm wind off the Arkaroola washed over her body and she lifted her arms over her head and felt the country all around, everywhere, stretching out to the horizon, reaching in right here to the point where she was standing, pressing in on every side. How quiet the land felt that night, yet also seething, full of things she had no names for, has no names for. If she had names she would be able to hold this feeling more snugly in her memory, carry it with her on her journey, round and intact.

'Ten euros,' says the proprietor in French. 'For use of the booth.'

He holds out his hand, the nails bent and yellow. In English he continues, 'Maybe no connection but a long time.'

She studies the posters of the footballers behind his head and waits for him to change his mind.

He keeps his hand cupped on the counter.

'Cinq euro,' she says, and places a five-euro note on the counter.

'Deux euro!' The bearded security guard is suddenly back in the shop, shouting.

He throws his arms about, then props himself on the counter. There are French words in what he is shouting but Lise cannot understand him. The proprietor is shouting back. Their two mouths are open at the same time.

The proprietor flicks at the note she just gave him and it floats to the floor, out of sight. The guard puts his fist on the counter. The proprietor pings the till open, takes out a coin. The security guard gives the coin to Lise. Then he grasps her elbow, steers her lightly, and moves behind her out of the shop.

Huh huh, the proprietor drily coughs or maybe laughs, Huh huh.

She and the guard turn left, in the direction she came, towards Paris.

'I take you back to your hotel?' the security guard says in English. 'Make sure?'

She moves her elbow away from his cupped hand.

'I think I will hail a taxi,' she says in French. Then catches herself. She has said she hopes for a taxi. *J'espère que...* Would that be right?

There are no taxis to be seen. They walk on down the street together. Lise tries to think of something else, not this street, not the desperate man with the shadowy eyes, not this second man with the silver-leopard embroidery shining on his breast pocket.

She remembers Coupeau and Gervaise walking out together, in those days after Lantin has left, how they walk and walk, she without a goal in mind, he determined, sweet-talking, wearing down her will. It was summer then, the shadows short, as they are where she lives, always. She remembers Goujet too, with his blond beard, Goujet worshipping Gervaise, impressing her with his craft, here, somewhere, in his blazing forge behind these same wet streets.

It is properly dark now. There is a light drifting mist, no longer quite rain. It's not cold enough for her scarf. She undoes its knot. As soon as her arm comes back down from untying it, the security guard again touches her elbow. In fact he pinches her elbow, not hard, not tight, but with his fingers in a narrow pincer shape. His knuckles touch her ribs, graze her ribs almost. She pulls away, her feet sliding, but still she feels the pressure.

She thinks of Coupeau putting no pressure, yet putting pressure. She can step away at any minute. Any minute a taxi will come.

See what you can see, she tells herself again. She has made it here, it is enough. This is Paris, the Goutte d'Or, the Rue des Poissonniers, it must be, she must have seen the sign.

The soft mist is settling in her hair and on her sleeves. She is touched by the mist of Paris like Gervaise will have been touched, or Virginie, or Nana, the wet silvering their hair, the flowers on their bonnets, and Goujet's beard, and Lantin's top hat.

She holds her free sleeve to her mouth and tastes the beads of wet, their woolliness and their coldness, and feels herself smiling at the silliness and the insanity and the coming together of all this, the mist and her books and her dreams and the sounds of the traffic here on the very long Rue des Poissonniers running south, north like her highway at home.

The man adjusts the position of his hand on her elbow. He's still here! She takes a longer step, more of a jolt than a step. The droplets on the edge of her hood fall like silver beads. But still she feels his thumb on the outer bit of her elbow and his fingers on the inside, against her ribs.

Someone catches up with them and passes close by and

overtakes—a tall man, but not the man in the denim jacket, she's sure. Still, her fear comes back, dries her mouth. In the mist it's difficult to make sure.

She falls back into step with the guard. At some point a taxi will come, she tells herself. *J'espère que...* It is Paris. There will be the yellow light of a taxi saying *Libre*. When she sees it she will have to raise her hand very quickly. If it is travelling in the wrong direction, north, it will make a big loop. Then it will draw up alongside, pointing south, and she will quickly drag open the door, free her elbow, throw herself into the back seat. She will not say goodbye.

At the thought of the taxi and its friendly yellow sign she feels suddenly in tune with these pedestrians, the guard and all these others, their bowed heads coursing down this long street shining in the wetness. She and these others, they are flowing in a single current, neither left nor right, the drizzle lightly drifting and glittering under the street lights overhead and the mist cold on their lips.

And then she knows for sure that something in her life that once gaped open has been filled—in fact it's brimming with ice-blue light, it's flowing smoothly forward like a tide into this present instant, it's welling up through the cracks between the paving stones and it's bearing on its breast eucalyptus leaves and bits of wiry twig and curling bark and the smell of diesel and desert sand and the reflection of a traffic light turning red to yellow to green without a single car passing.

A taxi suddenly draws up, its yellow light shining on her boots. Lise wrenches open the door, the security guard still beside her, holding onto her elbow.

'Rue de Rivoli, the youth hostel,' she jerks away. 'Merci,' she says into his dark-brown eyes, 'Merci, merci, merci.'

To the Volcano

THE FIELDTRIP PLAN kicked off that hot winter's day with a rumour shared over the 3.30pm tea trolley in the staffroom. Later, no one could remember if it was Bob Savage the cultural critic or the geologist Sid Duncan who had mentioned it first, the old extinct volcano a few miles off the highway to the north. Or perhaps it was Eddie Adams, the new lecturer in environmental history, who had said something in passing while admiring the laden tea trolley.

'One of the wives?' Eddie asked, looking at the outsize teapot, the Marie biscuits on their floral plate, the cake tin full of fresh coconut-ice slices and cherry buns.

'Our usual modest but surprising Thursday spread,' someone had said, probably Danie Price the statistician. 'We owe it each time to one of the wives. They do the baking.

Thanks to them our teas are pretty good out here, considering, you know, we're a further-education college out in the sticks.'

'One of the wives?' Eddie asked again. It was her first Thursday tea-time and she was trying to get acquainted. 'So, does that mean I should bake, too, one Thursday? I don't have a wife.'

But no one paid attention. They were listening to Bob, who had just said something about magma. Bob was a one-time Shakespearean who now worked on celebrity icons like Monroe, Guevara, and logos of global interest, the Apple apple, for example. Volcanos, though—they were something else, Bob said, powerful symbols, sure, but actually the real thing, too. Magma was pretty dangerous, pretty real.

He scratched the air with his fingers when he said 'real thing', the fingers not holding the cup. He'd heard about the old volcano from his neighbour, a hiker with a side interest in seismology.

'Today little of the crater is left,' said Bob, 'What we see are mainly the magma pipes—they're like the volcano's plumbing, millions upon millions of years old.'

'Rings a distant bell,' said Sid Duncan, catching his tea-softened Marie biscuit on his tongue before it broke. 'It will be one of the few dormant volcanos we have this far south. I've never seen it, but it's in the textbooks.'

Eddie turned away from the tea trolley and, as it was her first Thursday tea, tried again to step into the conversation.

Yes, she ventured, talking to the wall, a bell was ringing for her too. Her boyfriend Jamie—her on-off boyfriend the barfly Jamie, she might have said—had met a trucker once. He was always talking to truckers. The trucker had this story of an ancient crater far out on the savannah to the north. The locals avoided it, he said, it was a bewitched place.

'That's what I also heard, it's ancient and it's bewitched,'

Bob turned to her, grateful for her interest. 'Nearby, you wouldn't know it was there. When you pass by, my neighbour said, it looks like no more than a low hill, rubbed back into the landscape. But when you go over the top, they say, into the crater, it's another world.'

'Jamie said it was where a meteor struck,' Eddie poured herself a second cup of tea. 'He said the crater is an impact crater, not a dormant volcano.'

'It's definitely a volcano, long extinct,' Sid said sharply. Who was this young woman to know anything about it? Environmental history wasn't even a proper subject. He remembered her boyfriend, the longhaired guy at the start-of-year party who'd put out his cigarettes in a plastic cup of wine. 'If we were there I could show you, all of you. The land folds around the rim of the crater, indicating the long-ago volcanic activity.'

'The idea of a field trip impresses itself irresistibly upon me, colleagues,' said Bob, suddenly excited, ruddy. 'Open to students in all subjects. There won't be a crush. Most of our students don't know what field work is. They have no idea. They think geography is elsewhere and history is elsewhere. And they wouldn't be far wrong. Culture is certainly elsewhere. Even the transition feels like it happened in another country. But this history is close by, it's there for the viewing. Let's do it—a proper field trip, a talk by Sid on the coach, lunch boxes, the whole package.'

'Hire us a bus, Sid,' said Texas Mpe the lab technician. The whole time he had stood smoking silently at the open door. He was allowed, because he was still the only black academic staff-member. 'We can make it a joint trip, senior students, perhaps a couple of first years, a good complement of staff. You'd get the history kids along, wouldn't you, Eddie?'

'If there was something to argue about, yes,' she said.

'Meteor crater over volcanic crater, that kind of thing. Earth history from above and below.'

The plans were in place by the time the Marie biscuits and coconut-ice slices were eaten. They pinpointed Friday week. Sid contacted the coach company before he went home that afternoon. Bob phoned the college principal who straight away gave his blessing. The principal mentioned a hitherto undisclosed funding pot earmarked for field trips. He regretted he could not himself make it. Eddie put up a poster on the history noticeboard calling all interested students.

At morning tea the next day Bob left a sign-up list on the trolley—eight staff places only. When it was almost full, bar one place, he gave the list to his wife Sue to type up. She left an underline for the extra place. Everyone who had been around the tea trolley that day had decided to come, plus a colleague in Sid's department—Arnott Sergeant, an earth scientist.

Texas offered to get t-shirts printed with the words *Volcanic Fieldtrip* or something similar, but there was no time to push through the order. In any case, only Refile Masimong the communications officer had shown interest in the t-shirts and the admin team wasn't officially invited on the trip.

'I'll have a yellow one, Tex,' Refile said, bumping into him at the staffroom door where she had no business. She lit her cigarette off his. 'I know about that crater, it's my part of the world, my stamping ground. I'd like a picture of it on my t-shirt smoking away, like this'—she blew a smoke ring—'not extinct.'

Then she caught his listening look and followed his gaze into the dark recesses of the staffroom. They saw people milling around the tea trolley, the list lying on it.

'Honest truth, Tex,' she said. 'I know that area. Ask those folks to have me along, what's to lose? I can tell stories about the place as we drive. As kids, playing, we always made sure the volcano ridge was behind us, where we couldn't see it. It weighs on you, you'll see. It's a powerful place.'

'Put down my name,' she persisted later in the smoking area outside her office, the place where they usually met. 'I can be the extra, the eighth. So what if there's no t-shirt? Just take me. Barley in accounts can mind the shop.'

At that moment Bob walked past in the direction of the car park. He nodded at Tex, then more slowly at Refile, a deep, slow nod.

'I'd say she comes along, Texas,' he said over his shoulder, then stopped and turned back. 'Refile, isn't it? You can write up the trip for the newsletter. Get Texas to put your name on the list. There's a place waiting for you.'

~

The group gathered around the coach early that Friday morning. Though the sun was up, frost still sparkled on the ground. Refile had printed out the day's weather stats on a sheet of A4. Her first job each day was to send around a local weather report by college email. Today she had printed out a copy.

19°C/7°C. Sunny. Wind 8 mph from the south. Humidity 29%.

Holding on to the paper with cold hands, she squeezed her way through the students clustered at the coach door. Sid Duncan was talking to the group, handing out a fact sheet.

She clambered in and found Bob already sitting in the front seat behind the driver. She stuck the weather report on the glass panel between them, then took a seat across the aisle. She watched Bob read her notice.

'The weather stubs give me starting points for newsletter stories,' she folded her arms inside her anorak. 'I don't like the sound of that cold south wind, though. It's an ill wind...'

'There'll be no wind in the crater,' Bob looked at her levelly. 'You go over the rim, I'm reliably told, and it's a different world. In there, it's always summer.'

'I know,' said Ref. 'I know the area. And I say, bring it on. Growing up, we never went to the volcano. It was *zwifho*, so our parents forbade it.'

~

By the time the field-trip party reached the grassy area at the base of the volcano, it was nearly noon. The reports had been correct. The crater ridge was low and long and difficult to discern even from a few miles' distance. They had to stop every so often to get their bearings and each time Sid needed Arnott Sergeant's help to trace out the crater's shape. Close to, the road curved unexpectedly around the ridge and approached from the north.

Refile had slept all the way, waking up dehydrated when the driver turned off the engine. She found her head pillowed on Bob's folded jersey.

'I hope you don't mind,' he said from across the aisle, holding out a bottle of water, 'I couldn't stand to see you sleeping without a support for your head.'

'I missed giving the guided tour,' she said, frowning, cricking her neck.

Getting lost was the order of the day, Refile later wrote in her newsletter article. Confusion too, getting confused. Three parties went into the crater, and four returned, in different groupings from those that went in. No one got back at the agreed time. All brought different stories. Some spoke of scrubland, others of lush grass and willows, others again of a reedy lake, a kind of vlei, you might even say billabong, yellow-green in colour. But everyone spoke of a weird other world, iridescent green, windless, sweltering, silent—without birds, without cicadas, with no animal tracks in evidence at all.

The driver alone did not enter the crater. He stayed with the coach and did not appear in Refile's article. Once his last passenger had climbed down, he locked up, stretched himself under an acacia and went to sleep. He slept until Eddie and Texas woke him. They were the first people to return.

His mobile phone held high in the air, Sid led the first group into the crater with Arnott beside him. Sid's group was the largest and included most of the students. Four stayed back with Texas to have a smoke. Sid pointed out various features as they climbed—that concentric fracturing, these 'onion ring' rocks of different ages.

'You've got to imagine this as a great old navel in the ground,' Sid said, turning to the students and throwing open his arms. 'Imagine the mighty mountain that once stood here rearing above us, its top aflame. What you see now is the worn-down base of what stood here then.'

The second party left the grassy area with Bob at its head and Eddie bringing up the rear. At first, Refile had rushed to catch Sid's group, wanting to make notes from his commentary, but they were going too fast, so she joined the second. She sat on a rock waiting for them and wrote Sid's image of the great old navel into her notebook.

Texas hung back, hoping Ref might dawdle also, pause for a smoke. But then he spotted her yellow top receding up the slope and turned to gather together the third group, the smokers, Danie and the four students. They took their time walking up and entered the crater over a low declivity that gave a view onto grassland stretching down to reedy water, mirages dancing in mid-air.

From here, they saw Sid's group making a zigzag line through the thorn scrub, and Eddie standing at the vlei's reedy edge, beside a clump of willows, shading her eyes against the glittering light coming off the water. Ref's yellow top was nowhere to be seen.

Texas remembered this view later, on his way back. He had

split away from the smokers and ran into Eddie scrambling over the crater's edge.

'Have you seen Bob?' she asked. 'He got out of breath and we left him resting in some shade, but now he's no longer there. Or we've been searching around the wrong trees.'

They waited till the whole group had gathered back at the coach—Sid and the students, the stragglers from what had been Bob's party, the smokers' group now joined by Refile. She had seen them leaving the crater and followed them out. She volunteered now to go back in to find him.

'I found some good shade by some willows,' she said, 'He's most likely there.'

Texas followed her for a distance, but she went too fast. He remembered that she knew the area, she grew up here. He watched her crossing the crater's edge, dark against the white late-afternoon light.

Refile returned with Bob leaning on her arm, his hands in hers. It didn't take too long now, did it? she said. He'd been by the willows all along, just as she'd thought. He was waking up as she arrived, a little sunburnt and confused but basically fine.

Sid and Eddie shepherded the students on to the coach.

'You were talking about the willows, weren't you, Dr Savage?' Ref said gently, guiding Bob to the coach door. 'Willow, willow, you said. You think willows give good shade?'

His foot on the first step of the coach, Bob grabbed hold of her arm and looked into her face.

'I have had such a dream,' he whispered. Refile put her finger to her lips but he ignored her. He had repeated these words many times all the way down the ridge. 'I have had a dream and a most rare vision, lady. And I would sing it to you, for you were in it.'

~

'It was like stepping into another world,' Eddie said in the bar that night, her face aflame with sunburn, 'Really. The minute you went over the crater edge.'

'Made by a meteor,' said her boyfriend Jamie.

'Made by whatever. You clambered in, not really noticing much at first, you had to watch your step on the rocks and the path went down steeply, and then suddenly it was five degrees warmer and the wind died away. It was so green in there, radioactive green, with different plants than on the outside. Succulent plants, tangled.'

'A lot of divisive energy in craters,' Jamie stared into his beer, 'Impact or explosion.'

'That's right,' Eddie said, and threw her scorched arms suddenly around him, drawing him close. 'The weirdest thing was, we all immediately lost each other, the scrubland was so dense. The second you got left behind, you were lost. I was in a small group and we thought we were kind of contained, held inside the crater, but we were quickly separated. We wandered around in circles for hours.'

Jamie shifted on his barstool, releasing the lock of Eddie's arms.

'The more I hear, the more I think your lot must be right,' he said. 'It's a volcano crater, not from a meteor. I'd like to see it. What do you say that next weekend we take a bottle of tequila, drive over there and get wasted? See what happens. Maybe we'll feel something, hear the ancestral spirits singing from the vlei—'

'I say we don't, Jamie.' Again Eddie threw an arm around him, again he shifted away. 'It's not a place to get wasted. On the trip one of the lecturers became unwell. We didn't know what to do to help him. He was beside himself. He rambled all the way home, reciting Shakespeare. In fact, I've been thinking I should call the people who looked after him, Refile, Texas, check how he's doing.'

'Babe, I don't want you to phone those folks,' Jamie caught the bartender's eye, pointed to his empty glass. 'Within minutes you'll invite them over. You know how I hate it, socialising with your colleagues. If you want, you can do your calling and I can head off someplace else. Or I can get you another drink and you can put your phone back in your bag.'

~

When Bob Savage got home that evening, he left his car parked in the drive and went in to shower, pack and write two letters. The first letter was to his wife Sue, the second to Refile, his beloved. He took paper and pen from Sue's desk, the top drawer neatly stacked with stationery. He left his overnight bag at the front door, ready to pick up as soon as his letters were written. He had booked himself into the Holiday Inn, the one across town, closer to the college, closer to where he guessed Refile lived.

As on most Fridays, Sue was out at a City Hall recital with two of her friends. She'd be back within a couple of hours, Bob knew, and he wanted to be open with her. He wanted to write a frank letter and let her know their life together was at an end, he could endure it no longer, this life out of touch with his true feelings, this rip-tide of love and desire now sweeping through his veins.

My dear Sue, he began. *Please don't be concerned. I am going away for a few days—*

He stalled. There were no words for this fever that possessed him, this great heat coursing through his body. He could feel the skin on the side of his face that had been turned to the hot winter sun blistering. His group had left him sleeping in the shade beside the reedy vlei and he had awoken with his face in the sun, burning, but not only with the sun. For such a creature had come to him as he slept, such a divine vision with eyes aflame, cupping his shoulders in her hands, drawing his head into her lap—it was with her fever that he burned.

Bob turned now to the second letter and the pen in his scorched fingers moved again.

The opening lines he had chanted in his head all the way home in the coach, his beloved's hand in his, her palm pressed to his palm.

My dear, my beloved, he wrote, *I want your fire filling me. I want your flaming spirit living within me as it did in my dream. In my life I have taken many wrong paths but now I see the way. You showed me the way when I awoke in your lap and looked into your fiery eyes and saw that my dream was reality.*

~

Refile cut up Bob's letter immediately after reading it that Monday morning following the field trip. He had posted the letter in her college mailbox. She sliced the paper into thin strips, saving the strips that had the best lines. Then she put the filleted paper in the toilet and flushed till not a piece was left. She didn't want anyone to find the letter yet some of these beautiful words she could not throw away. No one had ever written her such beautiful words.

Later, she stuck the strips into a scrapbook. When Texas moved in with her at the end of the winter, she hid the scrapbook in a shoebox in her college office, to keep them private. Bob was in enough trouble with the police without people finding out about the letter, too.

The night after the field trip Bob had been caught breaching college security, climbing over the front gate. He had worked his way through the razor wire across the top and forced the lock to the mailroom. He had left his blood on the gate, his fingerprints everywhere and his car slewed up on the concrete verge by the night guard's hut. The guard had been out on his beat.

Hours later the guard found Bob wandering in the waste ground beyond the college, raving, his limbs swollen with sunburn. Even in the police car he went on talking about relish sweet and manna-dew and a most rare dream he'd had. *I would sing it to you, lady, for you were in it*, he told Refile on the phone from the police station. He begged her to come to him as she had come in his dream, in her yellow shirt, pillowing his head in her arms.

~

'Great navel: Our trip to the volcano.' Refile's article in the college paper the following week was marked anonymous, but then so were most of the news stories the communications team produced. Everyone knew the likely author. The story opened with the same details of the weather that Ref had pinned up in the coach.

On Friday 3rd, a dry sunny winter's day, 19°C/7°C, the story ran, the college set a new trend when eighteen students from several departments together with eight staff embarked on a field trip to visit a local site of geological interest, the extinct volcano on Ngona Plain. Dr Sid Duncan guided the student party into the crater and discussed various notable features including the onion-ring fracturing around the edge. Senior students carried out independent research by taking readings of the microclimate in the crater's base.

The article concluded with thanks to Dr Sid for the guided tour and to Dr Bob, our expert on cultural icons, for suggesting the field trip in the first place, an excursion to perhaps one of the most iconic geological formations in the world, the volcano, which however had appeared on the day, to quote Dr Sid, as more like a great navel set into the landscape.

Directly below the story was a short notice.

Dr Robert Savage was unfortunately on sick leave as of

this week. His classes were suspended until further notice. His dissertation students were forthwith transferred to Dr Eddie Adams in History.

~

Later, long after the police enquiry into Dr Savage's break-in had presented its report, Refile sometimes read back through her newsletter article about the excursion to the volcano and shook her head over it. She was reading it tonight while Tex grilled minute steaks for their supper. She kept most of her articles in neat plastic folders here in this box-file. Discontentedly she riffled through it now. She was the communications officer, she prided herself on her skills, there were offers of promotion in her email inbox, but here in this article she had succeeded in communicating almost nothing—in fact less than nothing.

At the time she had thought the idea of the different stories would be effective—the groups bringing back different reports of the scrubland, the willows, the vlei. It was a catch-all device, it helped her summarise, give a picture of the party fanning out into the crater along different pathways, but it wasn't true, it hadn't happened, she had made it up. She had no idea where the different groups that day had gone. Everyone so quickly got separated. She herself soon lost her group. They had left her behind writing her notes, they had left Bob behind. The volcano might have been in her stamping ground but she had walked in the scrubland for what felt like hours, following disembodied voices and locating no one. She had found her way out only when she saw Sid's group crossing the crater's ridge.

'But that's the point, né, about your piece,' Tex came in from the kitchen unscrewing a bottle of chilled Sauvignon Blanc. He stood it on the table. 'It was just a story, a report, it wasn't meant to say anything important.'

Ref put out her tongue at him, closed the box-file, pillowed her head on her arms. Her left eye was throbbing in a way that meant a migraine was brewing. She wished she could go to bed and skip Tex's meal.

The lines she had cut out of Bob's letter ran through her memory, they came without effort. They had been true, truer than her article.

You have lit a fire in my soul, my beloved. My heart is as a bed of molten lava. My love is strong as death, its flashes are flashes of fire.

To this day, she had not shown Bob's letter, or what remained of it in her secret scrapbook, to a soul—not to the police, not even to Tex. It wasn't just that the letter counted against Bob when so much already condemned him. It was that she loved his lines, she genuinely loved them. And they were hers. He had given them to her.

Something real had happened to Bob that day at the volcano and he had found the words for it, words that rose from his heart. For this she admired him. *You have lit a fire in my soul,* he had said. Remembering, she felt her cheeks grow warm. Though it had ended badly for Bob—the sacking passed off as early retirement, the time spent in the psychiatric hospital on the coast—still he had found something true to say.

His wife Sue had at least stayed with him, Eddie had said so. Eddie had whispered the news to Tex over afternoon tea and cake. Around the tea trolley no one mentioned Bob's name out loud but they missed Sue's special coconut-ice slices. Bob and Sue had moved to a duplex development out of town, Eddie said. Some weekends she went to visit them.

As for her, Refile, she had written her article and yet the things that counted that day were missing from it, all of them— the dead still air and the still reeds where no birds sang and the man asleep on the vlei edge opening his eyes in wonderment, *My beloved, I see you.*

Something had come to her out there in the crater, Refile knew, it had brought on these migraines—she had never had them so fiercely before. But she had not captured it, this thing that had happened, and she had not understood it. A perception had come, there it was, drifting in the still air, slowly, slowly, within view, within earshot, but she was looking elsewhere, and, ah, it was gone, she had missed it. She had missed her moment.

O my love, let your love not come too late, Bob had written, *for mine is a dark storm breaking out of season.*

She lifted her head. She sensed Tex was looking at her. He came over now and put his hand to her forehead.

'Eh, man, Ref,' he twisted one of her braids around his fingers. 'You need to start forgetting that old white guy. He belongs to another planet, another time. He's not worth worrying about, not like this.'

'He isn't but he is,' said Ref. 'You see, I can't lie, it was the things he said, I can't forget them. Something crept into his head that day he slept in the crater and it changed his life. He gave way to it, he let it change him. Who else can say as much?'

'It changed his life, sure. He lost his job, he lost his mind, he nearly went to jail.'

'Maybe, but he said the most beautiful things. I wish I could say anything half so beautiful. I wish I could thank him properly for the beautiful things he said.'

Evelina

17.30

Evelina liked to hang around airports though, till today, she had never yet left one on an aeroplane. She liked to sit in the arrivals halls, in the coffee place close to the exit where families waited with balloons and smiles. She liked to absorb the *ambiente*. She was absorbing it now, though in departures not arrivals, in the café alongside the security gates, drinking her coffee and smiling as she watched the families smiling. It made her happy, that she could be included in their *ambiente*, though she wasn't required to say a word.

Her airport hobby had started a few years ago—three or four, she couldn't remember exactly, back in the old century— the day she said goodbye to her best friend Marta. After her marriage went bad Marta had decided to make a clean break. Evelina and Marta had sat here in the same café, Marta retouching her lipstick, peering with narrowed eyes into the clip-open lipstick case she always kept in her bag.

Evelina had watched Marta walk that day through the departure gates sobbing into a tissue but with a kind of skip of her left heel, a definite spring in her step. Watching Marta's departing back, Evelina couldn't help noticing the spring.

These days Marta was teaching languages in Spain, near Toledo. She was earning good money and seeing someone, she wrote, a nice teacher at the secondary school. Although she worried sometimes that he was so much shorter than herself, worried what their future children might think.

Their other friend, Teresa, mouthy Teresa, took the same exit route a year or so later. Again Evelina came to say goodbye. Again she bought a round of hot chocolate here in the café, and again stood with her face pressed to the security glass, watching Teresa sink down the long escalator to the departure gates, Teresa waving and smiling and then, as she stepped off the escalator, quite briskly tucking her tissues away in the side pouch of her bag.

Teresa had aimed to join Marta in the language school in Spain but then she had got talking to people, and people had talked nicely about her, so now she was working on cruise ships in the Caribbean. Everything had changed for her and was raised up to a new level, and now, Teresa wrote in her last birthday card, it should be Evelina's turn. Now Evelina had her chance to go away like the others. She should grab the opportunity in both hands.

By the time Teresa left, Evelina was already in the habit of coming to the airport. She came perhaps once a month, especially on quiet weekdays, in the evening, sometimes still in her tour-guide uniform. The only person who knew about her habit was Jorge himself. She liked coming even without anyone to wave off, perhaps more so. She liked having time to watch the families, the kids in their Brazil-made *chanclas* running and chasing each other around the chairs and tables like these two little girls about six or seven here at the table beside hers. Round the table they chased, now one way, now the other, the smaller one giggling helplessly. She liked it so much she sometimes skipped going over to stand in the departure area, though she liked it there, too, watching the travellers being hugged.

But her best bit, secretly, was her own private *regreso*, coming back into the city after her airport coffee. This she liked the most. Sitting at the airport *and then* coming home again. She liked swooping her car into the fast lane, nearly empty at this hour, and then up the steep ramp and down her own *avenida*. She liked that feeling of coming back into her tiny flat, up the three flights of concrete steps that the janitor washed at five every evening, and opening the door onto her two neat rooms with everything standing exactly where she had left it. Even if that was just a few hours ago and no one could possibly have been in.

How grateful this journey made her for everything that she had here in this city. Which is why she couldn't get enough of visiting the airport, that heady feeling that the trip back home gave her every time.

Her family didn't know about this habit of enjoying the arrivals hall or they might have come along on this mild Saturday evening, to help her get away, to give her the push she needed.

Her parents lived up country now, in the campo. They had held their send-off last weekend in her flat—her parents, her older brother Enrico who was a small pets vet, a couple of cousins from her mother's side. They had made the four-hour round trip together in Enrico's car. She had served oozing *facturas* from the *panadería* downstairs, and black tea with lemon, plus stronger stuff for those who wanted it, and they had all talked about the repairs to Enrico's new house and when he might start converting his extra garage into a practice. One of the cousins would be coming to stay for a while in Evelina's flat, to have a long-expected holiday in the city, they said. They had talked only about solid things. As if by not saying much about Evelina's leaving or about Jorge, the reason for her leaving, they could all pretend it wasn't really taking place.

On the washed concrete steps they had said goodbye and their hugs had been dry and unfussy. They were immigrant people, a little Welsh, a little Irish, and a lot of Buenos Aires. They set their faces to the future, which is to say, the future that was here, now, and solid.

From the beginning Evelina's father had refused to say Jorge's name. He had refused at first to meet him and, when he finally did, he refused at first to shake his hand. But he had never paid any of her few boyfriends even a morsel of attention.

'His eyes want to undress you,' he said of the first, Luciano, all of seventeen, still at school at the time. 'It's disgusting, *arrojalo*, get rid of him.'

Evelina had, but none of the others she brought home later had fared any better. Papá said he wanted to hit them all. In another day and age, he swore, he'd have taken a sword to them, pure and simple.

So this afternoon it was Evelina's turn to sit in the airport waiting for a plane, on her own, without her family, but this time with a ticket in her purse. It was her turn to begin a new phase, in North America, in New York, a new phase to go with the new century, a chance to explore a new life with Jorge her fiancé—her energetic, open-hearted Jorge who had gone on ahead to set things up.

Sitting in the departures coffee shop, smaller than the one downstairs, Evelina noticed for the first time the good view through the big window beside the check-in gates. Even from here she could see through the window a section of the runway and the lit-up planes criss-crossing like fireflies against the sky now darkening towards evening.

Next time she was here, she told herself, she would go over to the window to take a longer look. There was a shiny rail to lean on. There were people right now leaning on it, looking out, pointing, their dark profiles stamped on the glass. But then she remembered there wouldn't be a next time and she had to put down her coffee, her hands trembled so.

The bag of toiletries and warm clothes she had packed stood beside her. She kept her leg pressed against the bag and her handbag pressed between her feet. Their box crates had gone ahead. For the air trip itself she hadn't known what to pack. What do you pack when you are changing continents, setting out to make a new life in New York with your beloved, your *prometido*? You could pack everything, or you could pack only your most special things that you wouldn't want to send in a crate.

When her alarm rang this morning, she couldn't find anything special enough to take along, nothing anyway that was small enough to carry, so she packed just this compact bag and in the end put in the wind-up alarm clock itself, on top, wrapped in a hanky. Couldn't do any harm to start a new life with a reliable alarm clock.

As for the box crates, filling them had been like filling bags for charity, piling in stuff you never expected to see again. Even now, a few weeks on, she could barely remember the contents— Jorge's kitchenware, yes, with his special block of knives; a needlepoint picture of snowy mountains done by his late mother as a young woman; also a few old pieces of furniture, hand-me-down stuff dry and cracked from standing long years in the sunshine in relatives' apartments.

Old stuff for a new country—to her it didn't make sense but Jorge insisted. It would cost the earth, he said, beginning a new home in New York from scratch.

Evelina wished Jorge was here now to give the encouragement his bright face always sparked in her, not that she ever let on. She didn't want to raise second thoughts in his mind. She didn't want him to know how scared she could get. With his big voice, his big muscles, his strong stride—nothing gave him a way of understanding this tremble now in her hands.

Perhaps it wasn't wise for him to have gone ahead, she thought, though she had pressed him to go, so that he would believe in her. It wasn't wise, too, that she hadn't yet let out her flat, her little home in the big city with its *panadería* downstairs and the outdoors gym painted in rainbow colours across the street. Would she, would *they*, be able to find anything so well set up in New York?

Right now Jorge was staying in some cheap hotel trying to find them a new home. They'd talked through every detail. He'd said he'd get in touch as soon as something worked out but he hadn't yet called. She wished he'd called. She told herself he was waiting for her—waiting for this plane out there now on the runway, waiting for her to arrive in it, to come to New York to be with him and make a new home. She knew he would tell her everything then.

Home! Evelina looked around at the familiar purple sky beyond the window, and, closer at hand, the children in their flip-flop *chanclas*, two small boys this time kicking an empty drink carton back and forth—the little girls had disappeared. She looked at the shiny stickers of saints on the menu board over the coffee machine, and the two old men in crisp polo shirts talking at the exit, gesticulating just the same as they would meeting in a park in town.

Already these things were starting to look flat, two-dimensional and flat, as though they were already receding from view. Soon, within an hour or so, they would be pushed into the far distance by the whoosh of the aircraft, and then, tomorrow, by Jorge and his dreams, Jorge whom she really liked and thought she could soon, very soon, begin to love.

Jorge, she thought, and saw him sitting in front of her with his hair tumbling over his forehead just as he had sat right there across the table at this exact coffee place those weeks ago at this exact time, give or take, the two icy red *aperitivos* standing untouched between them. He had bought them *como una celebración*, he said, to mark the start of their big adventure together.

Jorge's pale eyes in his bronze face had searched hers for some sign of reassurance, she could feel the pull in them, and she had told herself silently sitting there with her hand in his that she would see him again soon, in only a couple of months, seven or so weeks, though it felt a lot longer. And she had wished, still silently, that it didn't feel so long.

'The planes for North America always leave around now,' he had told her, following her eyes watching the departure boards. 'Always in the evening,' he went on, 'so that when you arrive *es un nuevo día.*'

He had been making conversation, she could tell, thinking she knew these facts, but she hadn't really known these things. She knew nothing. She worked in tourism but she had never yet left the country, not in her whole life, not once.

All she did know was that every day around nightfall, wherever she was, she felt a pull to go home so strong it upset her to resist it. She had felt the pull then waiting in this café with him. She felt it now.

But how could she have told him this? It would have sounded like doubt. It *would* have given him second thoughts. Yet all she wanted right now, today, even on this day of her departure, was to be in her flat and draw the curtains and scrunch up in a corner of her armchair with a cup of something warm. She thought of her armchair, the red one her mother had given her, the armchair that right now, unbelievably, was making its way across the sea squeezed in a crate alongside Jorge's stuff.

'Now promise me,' he had urged that evening, his forehead shining like a lamp. 'When the day arrives, just lock up the flat, and come. We've sent everything ahead that we need. I'll be at the other end, remember, waiting for you. I'll take you back to our *apartamento*, the one I'll have got for us. We will start our new life. We'll marry as soon as. I'll begin straight away to get our paperwork in order.'

And Evelina had waved him off, watching him descend the long escalator, blowing kisses, till all she could see was his waving hand, and then, nothing. She had stood a while longer, in case he popped back into view. It was like him to step back, to give one last kiss, one last wave. But he hadn't. So, when she was sure he was gone, she had slipped down to the café in arrivals and ordered herself a coffee. Her mouth had been dry from something she couldn't place, though she knew it wasn't sadness.

Evelina now bought a second coffee, a takeaway, and wondered about going downstairs for a while, to the arrivals hall. It was still ages before the flight. But then she sat down once more at the same table in the seating area, and pushed her used cup and saucer over to the edge, to make room. She sipped her coffee and looked around at all the familiar things, the stickers of the saints, the stainless-steel bar, the children in their *chanclas* kicking and running. No one seemed to notice she hadn't paid the drink-in extra. No one bothered about her sitting here at all.

20.30

Evelina checked her watch and tucked her chin deeper into her cretonne scarf. The sky beyond the viewing window was dark now and the evening cool settling in, even here in this air-conditioned space. But she had come to the airport so early that there was still plenty of time. She had shifted now from the departures coffee shop to a row of angled chairs alongside it. There was more than enough time still to go through security and buy a bottle of water and an eye-mask at the other end, as Jorge had instructed.

'On the plane you make your own *refugio*, your own night capsule,' he had said. 'You tuck up in your seat and pull your blanket tight and close your eyes, and then, before you know it, you've arrived, you're there.'

'I know you,' he'd also said, just before he left, swallowing his *aperitivo* in one gulp and glaring in that unblinking way he had when he was concentrating. 'Don't sit around and think or you'll never be able to get away. Take your bag and walk straight through to the gates.'

Pressing her legs together and pulling her coat hem to her knees—her coat against the New York winter—Evelina tried now to bring his face into the very centre of her memory, to hold his image there so she could believe again in everything he had told her, in her new life in New York together with her handsome, savvy fiancé, believe in the restaurant business he would set up there, in a city full of restaurants.

But though he had sat across that table only a month or so ago the main thing she remembered was the pale eyes burning in his tanned face, that and what he said about the *nuevo día*.

When she arrives it will be the start of a new day.

Easier was detail from further back, the funny way his curly hair blew across his forehead when they went out cycling on Sundays, and their picnics in parks all over the city, and the food he liked to prepare, the curried eggs and spicy beef salads that were his speciality, the plastic dishes of food spread out along with his metal *mate* pot on her printed cloth on the grass.

She remembered their first date, at a rival steak restaurant to his, away from the centre, and the lovely loose feeling in her limbs that his energetic talk gave her, the pictures he painted of hiking in Patagonia, and seeing a mountain leopard, and then his dream of setting up a steak restaurant on Fifth Avenue. These details felt like just days ago.

Clearest was the very first time of course, that startling and magical day when they had first met. There he had stood at the city event for young entrepreneurs, talking and making gestures with his big arms. She had worked through the exhibition hall looking for him, trawling up and down the aisles, and had found him at last standing beside a poster that showed a steak *jugoso* in gleaming close-up, handing out leaflets, his fine wide face shining like a bronze mask.

Earlier, she had been at her post at the exhibition hall entrance just beyond the sliding doors and he had passed her. She had been in her brown-and-orange tourist-board uniform checking nametags and handing out convention maps. She had given him a map and he had been the only one to say *gracias*, politely, looking her in the eye.

She found his stall by remembering the number on his tag. For her whole break she stood and looked at him from beside a pillar. She had never seen anyone with so open a face, so confident and shining a look, the kind of face you'd travel halfway across the world to see again.

On his way out he caught her eye for a second time and she smiled.

'I saw your talk,' she said.

He wrote her number on the company card she gave him and called the very next morning, just before nine.

Their first date was that Friday and they had got to know each other quickly after that. He had taken her to film festivals all over the city to see the old Argentinian films, *BA a la vista*, *Rápido*, *La casa del ángel*. She liked the dusty smells of the art-house cinemas. She had only ever gone to big movie theatres before, with Enrico and his friends.

When Jorge proposed he took her back to the exhibition-hall entrance, to the exact spot where she had stood and given him her number. It was a windy day and old leaflets and other rubbish bowled about their feet.

Later, he said he'd invited a saxophonist friend to come and play them background music from *Rápido* there on the steps but the guy hadn't shown up. Who knows why? Jorge shrugged. Perhaps he hadn't given him enough money for the cab.

But it didn't bother her. She had her ring, she had his *declaración*. She assured him she preferred a proposal involving just the two people themselves.

Her father was more scornful and probably she shouldn't have told him. It wasn't his business. And yet she had blurted it out, there at her send-off party, the *dulce de leche* squeezing out of the pastry in his hand. And right away of course he harrumphed something about young men who thought too much about their grooming and too little about their bank balance. Which was unfair, she knew.

But she'd kept quiet, she'd said nothing in Jorge's defence. She'd merely turned her eyes away from Papá eating his oozing *factura* and remembered the Chinese burns he used to give her and Enrico as children, when they were naughty.

'See how much you want to stick to your silliness,' he'd say, wringing their arms like a rag, twisting harder if they squeaked.

'People go to New York and become anything they want— dancers, directors, professors, even princesses,' Jorge had said those weeks ago over their untouched *aperitivos*. 'It doesn't matter if you come from *los confines de la tierra*, New York makes dreams come true.'

'*Sueños*,' he had said, cupping one hand like a scale. '*Realidad*,' he had added, holding up the other.

She had looked hard then into his pale eyes. She saw in them excitement and hope. She saw the shape of the New York skyline. She would have liked to see something more, a little fear perhaps, so they could talk about that together. But Jorge's eyes were the eyes of a man who would forge ahead and press on regardless of what setbacks he might meet—a man who would build his dreams in the streets of New York even if he didn't have an Evelina to support him.

She jumped up now in a sudden impulse of horror, her coat falling to the ground. Jorge forging on without her, she couldn't bear to think of it. She must go through with this now, fly away or else! Or these extremities of the earth would swallow her up. Jorge had the power to save her. Jorge would fold her in his arms and make new things possible. He had hope enough for two. Her chance lay in his hands, no, in his hands *and* her hands. Tomorrow morning she would be with him, pressed to his side, travelling with him on the subway into the heart of New York. But getting there depended on her, on getting herself on that flight. That was it with fretting. She could lose everything this way. Her chance lay here in her hands.

She picked up her bags and saw there was still time, *un poco*, a bit of time. She checked her watch against the digital clock on the departures board and made her way over to the viewing window. She wanted one last look at the familiar sky, the familiar line of hills still discernible above the distant city, the planes with their illuminated windows ascending and descending. If she put it off now, she would not see it again for years.

21.00

The tannoy announced that the flight gate was open. Evelina turned from the viewing window and saw the clear bubble of the telephone booth on the near wall. She didn't want to see the booth but once she had seen it she couldn't forget it. One last thing she really had to do, this is what it was telling her.

Jorge hadn't called though he'd said he would, so now she would call him. Surprise, surprise, she would make a joke of it, laughing lightly. *Sorpresa*, little did you think! At the airport, where else? Just to say—this time tomorrow, our *nuevo día*, we'll be on our way home, beginning our new life together.

But what if there was no home, no new *apartamento*? What if their papers had been refused? She'd heard nothing. She put down her bags at the booth and checked the slip in her passport, the numbers he had given her, first his friend in the steakhouse business, and then his father's colleague's nephew. He'd be staying with either the one or the other, whoever had space.

'Don't call me, I'll call you,' he'd said. 'For a few days I won't have a phone.'

But he hadn't called. And it was weeks, not days. She didn't doubt him but still he hadn't called. Evelina felt suddenly empty, cavernous. She felt the great dark seas that separated them wash over her heart.

No, she thought, no, and reached suddenly for the back of the chair closest to her, the rough woollen shoulder of the gentleman sitting in it.

Somebody then took her arm and guided her to a nearby counter.

'You look very pale,' the attendant at the counter said. 'Look, why not give me your bags? I can help you to your gate.'

'Let me take a moment,' Evelina heard herself say in a composed voice. The cold steel edge of the counter pressing into her palm gave her comfort. It was like holding on to a raft.

'I was trying to make a call but somehow it didn't work,' she said. 'I didn't get through. Maybe I don't have the right number.'

22.00

The last call for her flight—for the second time they were calling out her name, *Evelina, Evelina,* as if they were welcoming her. She was on her way, she really was. She had worked in the travel business and now she was a traveller, too. She had made it through security and passport control. Her documents were here in her left hand, slid inside her travel company's own white plastic folder. The folder was her goodbye present from her colleagues, that and a smart purse containing a nail-care kit. Had she remembered to pack the purse? She wanted to check but as she made to bend down she caught sight of the gate number there ahead of her, silver numbers on a blue screen, and a flight attendant waving. There was no one else about, theirs was the last plane out and she was the last passenger to arrive. She was almost at the gate. Now it was just the flight bridge to go and then they'd seal the great aeroplane door behind her. She really was on her way. Tomorrow she'd be with Jorge in New York, riding the subway with him as they somehow had never done here in their own city, pressing herself to his side.

Jorge—she could see his pale eyes burning in his bronze face, his face like a mask sometimes, polished, shining. She tried to imagine him wav ing at her like the flight attendant was waving—waving across the great dark seas that stretched between here and New York. She made herself see the moving waters as if from high up in the dark sky, from the plane she would soon be flying in, soaring above those black waves she had so recently felt curling around her heart. From here up high, her seatbelt pressing into her lap, she could see, peering down, the stars reflected in the dark waters, and the lights of the city shimmering at their edge, and, though it was still night, the black arrow of the plane's shadow rushing across the moving, churning sea.

Blue Eyes

I

ALL JOHN CAN THINK right now is *hot*, so very hot, this noon light shafting unshaded into the letting agency's window. Hotter than the Mozambique hills in December, he thinks, hotter than lying all day in the sun behind a rock, waiting for the grunts to show themselves.

'No Rhodie ex-combatants for tenants, is the unofficial word,' the letting agent says. 'We can't discriminate of course, not when it comes to whites, but this is the bottom line.'

'But we're all enrolled here at the Varsity, Mrs… ,' John checks the raised stainless-steel name-badge on her desk, 'Mrs Villiers. We're all pukka students. *Ware* students,' he adds in Afrikaans for good measure.

'Yes,' his friend Mick beside him chips in. 'We didn't serve long, miss, not long at all. We were called up the day after our last school exam and demobbed a month and a half later. Before Christmas. It says there on the form. We haven't even had the independence celebrations.'

'We're even going to the independence celebrations,' John adds, mustering a lively voice, pulling his damp t-shirt away from his body. 'April. We're driving back up. Bob Marley is going to be there, everyone's going to be there.'

'I really do feel for you, boys, but there's no point going on trying,' the letting woman dips her chin into her scarf with its pattern of golden keys as if to draw in coolness from the silk. 'You want a home and, what's more, you're young, but, hey, you *were* soldiers, you can't deny it. That's why you're joining late.'

Mick in the cool of John's shadow is persistent. 'Guys here go to the army, too, Miss?'

'Look, it's what the landlords say,' the woman says. 'You Rhodie boys can't be trusted. You're drunk and crazy night and day. I'm not pointing fingers but still...I've seen you turn up in your dusty cars here on Main Street after two days on the road, rolling out blind-drunk like silly puppies, the driver included. *Zimbabwe Ruins*, the same as the words on your t-shirts. The landlords think you're mad as gnats. They think you'll rip their properties apart.'

John jerks his head in the direction of the door and Mick begins to shift on his seat. He reads John's face like John reads his. They are Rhodesian Special Forces brothers. They have spent every day together, every hour, from basic training on. Every night they slept side by side on their backs under the stars between the rocks, their FN rifles strapped to their fronts.

'Thank you, Mrs Villiers,' says John, shifting forwards also, getting up. 'You've been a great help.'

'My thanks to *you*, boys,' Mrs Villiers rises from her chair to shake their hands. 'Privately, of course, I can say how much we've admired all you did. The sacrifice you Rhodesians made, keeping the darkness back on behalf of us all. But that's privately. Here in the real world, well, you'll have to try to get on as best you can.'

'Sure, Miss, we will, you can bet on that.'

'Do what the other ex-Zim guys are doing, is my advice. Sign into the student dorm for a few weeks, go two to a room. Be good, put your Rhodie t-shirts away. Before long no-one will be able to tell you're not just us.'

The letting-agency door sucks closed behind the two and the February heat strikes them full in the face.

Not the Mozambique hills heat, John thinks, plucking at his shirt, not that heat that hits like a mallet, but the other heat that rose from the valleys, damp, soaking. There was a bit of breeze over the hills.

'Did I hear right?' he turns to Mick. 'Did she say we'll turn into South Africans before long?'

Mick begins to laugh and drags him out of sight of the letting agency.

'What's so funny?'

'*Zimbabwe Ruins*,' Mick reads off John's shirt. 'I hadn't twigged. She was reading the fuckin' words on your chest.'

II

The girl approaches from behind Mick—a tall reedy girl in tight faded jeans, a head taller than John and as thin as a skeleton. The two boys are still laughing.

'Hello,' she says. 'My name's Patty. You must be Rhodesians. I like Rhodesians.'

'Then we'll like you,' says Mick, always quickest with the girls.

'Which is more than we can say about some people round here, Patty,' John adds.

'Meaning...?' Patty says, and hands round her pack of Stuyvesants. The boys help themselves.

Within moments their story is out—their arrival yesterday from up north, the twelve-hour drive in convoy through their empty, war-scarred land, and then the twenty-four further hours from Beit Bridge. And now they are sleeping in their car with nowhere to stay, no place at the inn, Mick explains, *literally*, not even at the university, though they've enrolled. Everywhere is full up.

In the blink of an eye Patty makes her offer, 'Come stay at my house.' Her dad's her landlord, she explains, the owner of her small one-bedroom bungalow, and he lives a thousand miles away. There's a sofa in the passageway, and the passageway is wide. They can take it in turns on the floor. There's even a girl, a maid, Iris. She does the cleaning, cooking, everything. And Patty's car is parked right here. Look, no obligations, come take a look.

'How can we repay you, Patty?' John gets into her passenger seat. Already he knows he will take up her offer. He hears Mick slide into the back.

Patty gives John a skew look and stubs her cigarette out on the pavement with the heel of her sandal.

'In any case, let's introduce ourselves,' she says, closing the car door. 'This is what you need to know about me. I smoke like a factory, meaning all the time, so you are forewarned. I like to eat chewing gum. I swallow chewing gum when I've finished chewing it. I don't study much, but I do play music, piano—I'm here to do music. I'm a dunce at theory. Most of the time you won't even see me, I practise all day in my department. My dad offered to buy an upright for the house but I said no. I like playing the grand pianos in the department. Now, how about you two? Was your war bad?'

John thinks of his Mom's upright on the farm, the lid stuck

closed with damp and lack of use. He remembers his parents saying goodbye—just three days ago, was it? He sees them waving tight-lipped from the verandah, dropping him into the future for the second time in four months like a penny into a well. He says nothing for a bit.

'Our war was just six weeks long, Patty,' Mick is saying. 'We were the lucky ones. What can happen in just six weeks?'

III

John doesn't sleep at all that first night at Patty's, in Patty's bed. Whenever he is inside her Patty makes small cries, like a tiny trapped creature, sometimes even when he is not moving.

'You OK, Patty?' he asks once or twice. For a while she goes quiet, then resumes her cries.

They begin the evening on the concrete steps under the washing line in Patty's sandy backyard with a box of red wine. 'To housemates,' they cry out fiercely, clunking their glass mugs. They move on to a bottle of red in the kitchen, though by then Mick is asleep. They drag him onto the sofa in the passageway and return to the kitchen.

'You hungry, John?' Patty sways in front of her near-empty fridge, holding on to the door. 'Iris usually prepares food for me and leaves it here, but she's been away. Sick child or something.'

John reaches in behind her, lifts out the eggs from the bracket and scrambles them on the gas cooker. Patty eats noisily and fast.

'Come,' she looks at him thoughtfully and licks her wine-stained lips, 'tonight you can come share my bed. After your long drive south the floor isn't fair.'

She stands beside her bed and peels off her clothes without ceremony. He is surprised at her givingness as well as her thinness, the boniness of her buttocks as he pulls her towards him.

'Do you eat anything besides eggs and chewing-gum?' he asks.

'No, Blue Eyes John', she says, sliding down beside him. 'Did you know you have the bluest eyes I've ever seen?' She pulls herself on top of him, 'Bluer than my dad's. It's the kind of blue eyes that show up blank in the old black-and-white photos. You know, photos of the colonial days, lion hunts and that.'

'I don't want to think about my blue eyes,' John kisses her.

'I don't either,' says Patty. 'They're a weird blue. In the photos the men's eyes look washed out with acid.'

'Blue eyes gave us away in the bush. In the war. When we had black camouflage on.'

'I love it that you were in the war,' Patty kisses him back.

Later he lies wide awake staring up at the ceiling. He sees the endless road they've just driven zipping open the darkness, the thin ribbon of laterite and red earth running on and on to the horizon. Out on the passageway sofa Mick snores in his familiar, halting way. Patty's damp hair on his cheek smells of egg.

At last, around six, John gives up the attempt to sleep. He slides quietly out of Patty's bed and takes a shower. Then he walks in to campus to begin his university life.

'John, John, stop, stop,' Patty calls the second night, shaking him. 'Stop shouting. You're making such a noise. Look, the bed's soaked. I'm going to have to change the sheets. Roll over now, help me do this.'

IV

A week since they first met Patty in the street, Mick gives notice. He tells John as soon as they get in from campus.

'Look, bra, I want out,' he says, standing beside the sofa in the passage-way. 'You're an item, you and Patty, and I'm a third. I've met some second-year Rhodies with a house, all mad and drunk—that's where I'm going.'

Panic crashes through John and he can't think to say a word. He shakes his head at Mick's offered smokes.

'So, what d'ya reckon?' Mick lights up. 'You can come and join me any time, you know. We can share a room. I'm used to your noise, aren't I, and maybe Patty isn't?'

Patty, John thinks, and can't for a second bring her face into his memory, only those small mouse sounds she makes in bed—that and the tapping of her fingers, her thin fingers always tap-tapping surfaces, silently playing regardless of what else she's doing, her eyes inward—he sees them now—listening to some score in her head.

He watches Mick stuff his things into his khaki-green army bag and wants to reach out, pin his arms down, stop him. He and Mick—how many nights apart since they first met on patrol? Maybe just one or two, nothing to speak of—that stormy weekend back in early December, the time Mick went home for his grandad's funeral, just those two days.

And then Patty, a girl he barely knows, and her mouse noises, on and on like a hinge in need of oil till he wishes he was anywhere but there sleeping with her.

'John, man, you should write it down,' Mick drops his voice. Iris the maid is whacking her broom against the skirting in the kitchen. 'My Psychology lecturer said yesterday. It's a way of getting rid of things, writing them down. You write stuff anyway. Write it down, the things you shout.'

'I don't know what I shout, Mick. I wake up and my throat is hoarse. But I don't know what I've been saying.'

'There are words, John—Go, or maybe No. Get Patty to tell you, hey, and then write the things down.'

'She wakes me up all the time, middle of the night, Mick, but I don't know what I've said. And then I lie there staring and can't back to sleep, and suddenly I'm petrified about everything, every little sound. Look, man, I'll say it straight, I'm gonna miss you. I wish you weren't going. But I get it.'

V

Patty's household is out of clean sheets. It is laundry day and Iris has hung Patty's damp and soiled sheets on the line—all the sheets Patty has each night this past week dragged off the bed and stuffed under the basin in the bathroom because the laundry basket is overflowing.

'Iris!' Patty shouts. 'You haven't washed the sheets, you've only hung them.'

Iris doesn't respond or, anyway, John getting dressed in the bedroom can't hear her. But he imagines her making that sucking sound through her side teeth he picks up when he walks past her sometimes, like a clicking sound in her language, but hissing, disgusted. *Ssss*.

'Put them in the bath, soak them,' Patty shouts again, 'I don't care. They must come clean.'

That sound from Iris, this time he really does hear it.

'But I pay you, Iris,' Patty lowers her voice to plead, 'and I say you must wash the sheets. Wash wash wash, you know, with hands.' John hears her pummel one fist with the other. 'I don't care what you say, but you can't say no. You must do your job.'

The sash window latch, thank God, is already open. John slides the lower frame noiselessly upwards and lets his body drop down from the ledge into the street.

VI

In the cool sound-proof room in the music department Patty plays the baby grand piano. She plays Debussy, Poulenc, the C sharp minor concerto, and when she's properly warmed up, Chopin, fluid music she can play without ever seeming to stop, her fingers moving over the keys like ripples in a river, on and on, so that her thoughts can't catch up, can't move fast enough, her thoughts about John's night-time cries of No or Go or maybe Gook. Listen, she wants to tell him as she plays, this music that runs faster than fear, faster than panic, listen how it sweeps us onwards, drags us with it, its ripples covering over the dark shapes that rise up from below, dimly disturbing the current.

VII

Noon. John is fast asleep in Patty's bed, naked, the soiled sheets bunched around his body. Iris comes in with her broom, at first banging a little, thinking herself alone, and then suddenly tiptoeing. Her nose wrinkles at the terrible smell.

'Ai,' she makes a sibilant noise through her side teeth, 'Sies tog, jou arme ding.'

Then she puts her broom down. She sits on the bed and puts her hand over his hand where it lies on the pillow.

He nuzzles his face towards her hand, butting his nose like a baby.

'Ai,' she says again, 'Ai, ai,' watching him closely. His eyelids flutter. She puts his hand down, takes her broom, and backs silently out of the room.

VIII

It is laundry day again. Iris pounds Patty's clothes on the washboard in the kitchen. In the bathroom the sheets lie in piles, a load under the basin, another load in the bath. Patty filled the bath with water before she went out. As if a bride in white satin has fallen back and immersed herself, glistening, in the water.

But in spite of Patty's insistence, Iris will not wash the sheets. She won't even talk about it. She will hang out the sheets for the wind and the rain to scald—see, she's hanging them out right now—but she will not wash them. Patty knows that she, Iris, always does her job and that this is extra. More than extra. Patty knows that she will do everything else. She will cook macaroni cheeses to put fat on Patty's bones like her father wants. She will wash all the clothes including *his* and iron them too. She will leave her sick child with her sister and clean the house top to bottom and sweep the yard. But she will not wash the sheets, she will not. *Sies tog.* She will not.

Bang, slap, slap. John lies reading on Patty's bed and hears Iris pounding his clothes on Patty's washboard.

Later he goes down to the Manchester store on Main Street to buy Patty a set of new sheets. The sheets last one night. The next day he strips the bed and gathers up all the soiled sheets in the house. He takes them to the laundromat. It's no bother, he says. He'll make sure to do this every other day.

'But it's miles away,' Patty grumbles.

'In a car no more than a stone's throw.'

'I pay Iris to keep the place clean.'

'It's no trouble at all.'

Iris says nothing one way or another.

IX

John sets up an old school desk in Patty's backyard under the shade of next door's loquat tree. He pulled the desk off a pile of builder's rubbish. At his desk he opens his exercise book and begins to copy out in longhand the books open in front of him.

Copying, he has found, is the best way of learning. He has stopped going to lectures now. In fact, he has stopped going in to campus, except for once a week. Somehow he can't concentrate on what the lecturers are saying. He imbibes great books instead by writing down everything in them, from the very first word onwards, page after page. He sees himself looking out at the world athwart these books as if they were a broken kraal wall, a sandbag rampart.

On Mondays, on his weekly university visit, he goes to the library. Each time he takes out two of the books listed on the photostat course list he was sent at demob camp back in December, when they heard the war was over and they would be coming to university after all. He works down the list in alphabetical order. If he likes a book, which is to say, if copying down the sentences for about a page or two suits him, he presses on.

So far he has copied pages of Hemingway and he has copied Orwell. He can't believe Orwell in Spain saw all these things he describes, the street-by-street combat, the treachery and the violence, and then produced these clean, clear sentences. He envies Orwell his sentences. The best way of reducing this envy is to write his words down and somehow possess them.

From the kitchen window Iris watches him. When he catches her eye and smiles, she does not smile back.

x

Patty is the finale act in her department's end-of-term concert. She needs a good portrait photograph for the programme, she tells her friends. She sets up the shot in the Botanical Gardens in front of a bed of aloes. She wears a white Indian dress with lacy sleeves and gold-thread tassels along the hem. Iris has specially ironed the sleeves. Patty's hair is back-combed and stands out from her head in a halo. She hands John her Leica and puts on a pair of Jackie O sunglasses. Mick stands by with his own small Kodak instamatic.

'You can lose the Polaroids, Patty, and the aloes,' says Mick. 'The sunglasses are too shiny and the plants are too spiky. You're the shiny, spiky, amazing thing people should be looking at in the photo.'

'I like the aloes,' says John, 'They make a good textured background. My photo was close up. I think it was good.'

'And I like the sunglasses, Mick,' Patty says. 'They give me John's blank look.'

'Glasses or no glasses,' says Mick. 'Let's just shift the angle and try that shrubbery as a background. It's green and beautiful, like when Patty plays.'

Patty stands in front of the shrubbery and throws back her glistening hair. Her thin arms are stretched above her head and the wind lifts up her lacy sleeves. She is so lovely that John forgets to take his picture.

'Just as well I brought a second camera,' says Mick. 'For my photo though, Patty, you lose the glasses.'

XI

The first time John is with Iris, he knows this. There isn't enough of him and still he is pouring himself into her, he is pouring everything he has. He is flowing into her till he is nothing but a husk, so wispy, so light, that she can gather herself around him, she can hold him as near and close as he has been to anyone, ever.

This close in, he can remember things, vague things. He can remember four in the morning, on patrol, and the white sheet lightning fading into the valleys, and then the running, everyone running—running, shooting, stumbling, running.

In the fitful white light he sees the guerrilla ahead run, then trip, fall, and he is standing over him, no her, *her*, the white lightning playing across her big glistening eyes, and the whipping wind booming *no no no*—

XII

Noon, and Iris has left her broom against the wall. Her uniform is caught up around her waist. She didn't have time to take it off.

'Open your eyes,' Iris says to John in English, 'Let me see you.'

He obeys. He looks into her eyes, she looks into his.

'Soos die see,' says Iris, 'Soos water sonder bodem.'

Like water with no bottom—John knows what she means.

XIII

'You fucked Iris,' Patty stands, arms akimbo, in her front doorway. John faces her on the porch. In his hands are two fresh library books. 'You fucked my black maid under my nose, in my bed, while I was playing piano, you fuck. You get out.'

XIV

'Look, I'm sorry, bra,' Mick sullenly flicks his nail against the door-handle of the car. 'You can give my ticket to someone else.'

'You sure?' John looks up at him. 'You're OK to miss it all?'

'If I came along, I wouldn't come back.'

'I'm going and *I* probably won't come back. Especially if you don't come along.'

'Man, something's gotta give. And I like it here.'

'I do, too, some of it.'

'Not as much as me. I don't think you'd ever want to come back, not even if there was something to come back for.'

'Who knows, eh, Mick? For now, I can only play it by ear. I'll go and play it by ear along with this whole list of Rasta men playing it by ear, playing the biggest sound system we've ever heard. I mean, forty thousand watts, did you hear?'

'Brother, you're right, you're right, you're so right!' Mick sings.

'Brother,' says John, 'how can I do independence without you? How can I drive all that way without you?'

'Just think of Marley's forty thousand watts,' Mick says.

'Biggest sound system south of the equator.' And he hits John's shoulder through the open car window.

XV

John drives. The sky ahead is blue with low white cloud banked up on the horizon and the sky behind is blue with low white cloud. A single condensation trail cuts through the blue, a line tracing west and south, to Cape Town or even farther—Tristan da Cunha, he imagines, Gough Island, South Georgia, Tierra del Fuego, places so far away they sound like myths.

A soaring bird bisects the white trail. He thinks of the birds of prey that surf the warm air currents over the Mozambique hills. They will still be there, coasting. He thinks of the fine balance of their wide wings. He thinks of Patty and her flying fingers. He wishes he could have heard more of the music that flowed from her flying fingers. He thinks of Iris. Of her fine skin and the tiny scars she has over her left eyebrow, of tracing them with his finger.

He thinks of his shame, the sheets flapping unwashed in the backyard.

Iris.

Perhaps he will never see them again—not Iris, definitely not Patty. To see them again he would have to come back, next month, next year, but in any event come back. Patty has said she will leave town soon, move on. She might play the cocktail hour in hotels in Port Elizabeth or East London. She is good at making fluid music, one piece sliding liquidly into the next.

As for Iris, her child will soon go to school, her child—Mongezi—who was sick but is now better. Iris will have to find another job to pay his fees.

John tests the thought of coming back. It fills him with neither grief nor joy. He thinks of the rage in Patty's eyes when he kissed her goodbye, a quick, dry kiss on her cheek.

He slides a Bob Marley cassette into the player.

'Brother, you're right, you're so right,' Marley sings.

Something about the voice decides him. The voice is all itself, like Orwell's voice. It has style, a measure. On this road running straight to the horizon, heading home, he wants to find a voice like that. Independence will bring a new measure and he must find a way of tuning into it.

Mick talked about artists returning to the country, frontline soldier-poets from the camps in Mozambique, avant-garde troubadours who till last week camped out in English meadows begging beer-money, all as mad and crazy as he, John, is, all biding their time of return.

John thinks of planeloads of poets in the sky and is suddenly impatient to be home. He fast-forwards the tape. 'No woman no cry.' 'One love.' He can't find the song he wants. In fact he doesn't know what the song is. He wants the two thousand miles that lie ahead to be behind him. He wants the Limpopo at his back.

The thunderstorm falls suddenly upon the car. The grey rain sheets thickly down the windscreen so he pulls over. He switches off the tape and lights a cigarette. The car is a cave of water that quickly fills with smoke. The lightning makes sparks of silver on the surrounding rocks.

Rain on wet rock, lightning, grey darkness. He remembers the Mozambique hills. He is there, as always, in the Mozambique hills.

He remembers her big eyes looking up, the gleams in her eyes from the lightning.

Her hands grip on his and he wrenches his FN back. Her eyes go brighter. She curls herself around his leg. She wants to pull him down into the mud, so he begins to kick. He kicks and he kicks. He kicks for a long time and then he bolts. In the distance his companions whistle for him.

He clutches the steering wheel and presses his forehead into its plastic till the skin begins to sweat. Iris, he moans, Iris.

As quickly as it came, the storm passes. The sky is blue again. He opens the car windows to let out the cigarette smoke and breathes in the smell of rain-stirred earth. He waits till his head clears and his heart stops pounding. Then he turns the key in the ignition. He pulls out onto the newly washed, blue-black road.

Powerlifting

KAY PUTS HER ELBOW to the screen door, balances her coffee mug. She shoves hard, then steps out on to her small brick porch in the shadow of the vine trellis. In her other hand is her transistor radio. The newspaper, still in its plastic, is under her arm.

Rod, when he lived here, never could believe how she managed to juggle things—juggle as in keeping two things in her head at once, double-thinking not just double-doing, multi-tasking. In point of fact it astonished him, considering how rubbish she was at most things—including mothering, in his opinion. That she could listen to the breakfast news *and* read the paper at the same time, this was a wonder. That she could take perfect case notes even while a suspect was yelling at her.

So, my one claim to fame, Rod, she would tell him, at least I have that. And thought privately, what's so special, keeping my focus on two strands of words at the same time—especially when it's generally the same news, the written and the spoken? As for the case notes, I'm writing what the suspect is saying, aren't I?

At other times, she told him, coffee is the magic ingredient, though it was never strong coffee.

Truth is, when she's reading, the radio here beside her on the wire-mesh table turns into white noise, padding the silence.

She is still in her pyjamas, non-matching top and bottom, rosebud design on top, cotton leaf-pattern trousers. Soon, in a few weeks or so, it will be too hot to wear long pyjamas to bed but, for now, it's comfortable. One of the joys of living alone, she thinks—not bothering one way or another, certainly not about night-gear.

Keeping her face in the shade, she stretches her legs into the lemonade-bright sunshine. Looks like it could be a good day—a good day with nice weather. For one thing, there's little to no news—which is to say, no news to worry about. For another, the magpies she heard yesterday are back, their liquid noises in the trellis overhead. And two white irises have bloomed overnight or, at least, she didn't notice them yesterday. And Donny just called, which is great for two reasons: because it's a special day for him, the date's been in her diary for months, *and* because it means that today she has spoken to someone. *Already* spoken to someone.

Since grouchy Rod, she prefers to speak to someone before going to work, to use her voice at least once or twice. She mentioned it in passing one day to Donny—I enjoyed talking to the magpies this morning—and maybe he took the hint. Talking clears away the night's cobwebs, brings her up to the surface of things. It gives a reality check, to put it in Donny's way. She needs to talk, to *do* talking.

This was the thing that killed her after Rod left, bad-tempered as he was, the main drawback of living alone. Arriving at work and having to clear her throat of accumulated silence as if a plug of mucus were stuck there and had to be coughed free.

Wish me good luck, Donny had said on the phone. He'd wanted her to know he'd arrived.

'There already?'

'Yes, where else, Mum? It's all happening in our own downtown arena, the National Powerlifting Championships. It's all totally real. I'm about to begin my warm-up.'

She pictures him in the arena locker rooms, stood beside the grey slatted lockers. She's handled an incident there before. He's unpacking his things—keeping apart from the rest, like his coach always tells him; drinking plenty of water like *she* always tells him.

From first impressions, he said, looking around, some of the other guys were huge, but not so much as to give him worries. A few he recognised from previous competitions. But he ignored them all. He sat and thought about his strategy. He knew he was better prepared than anyone.

Kay isn't sure what powerlifting *strategy* might be—doesn't it just involve hefting weights? But she's never asked and she doesn't expect him to explain. He is his own man now, presiding in his own coliseum, hailing his own crowds, today, on this very day, this afternoon. Highly commended the first year, then silver medallist two years in a row, and today—today, who knew?

She tucks her legs under, cooking now in their leaf-print fabric, something synthetic in the mix despite the *pure cotton* label. The light glitters on the newspaper in its plastic sleeve.

To think that Donny's just a few blocks over there, in the arena beyond the park and the cricket pavilion, ten or so blocks away—amazing. And still he phoned her, early as it was, when he knew he'd see her later. Medallist though he might be. He didn't even say, see you later. He knew of course she'd find a way to pop round.

Too soft to make it, Rod always said—mummy's boy, too soft for his own good.

Whatever that might be, Kay would silently retort. As far as she is concerned, men could use more softness. Something of the human touch could have helped Rod save his hardware business—that is, retain his personable, hands-on manager and so save his hardware business. Instead, he had ended up depressed and out of work, spending his days in the café down the street drinking free refills right up until the morning he finally walked out for good.

Softness definitely suits Donny, it complements his muscles, his bulgy chest. She takes credit for both, the softness and the strength.

Ignoring her aching heart, she has made Donny live away from home for over a year now. He hadn't wanted to go but by degrees she had nudged him away. She made him get his own toiletries, then clean his own shoes, then do his laundry, then find a room, though every push was hateful to her. It was like leaving him at nursery when he was a baby, walking away and hearing him scream.

Now and again she asks Donny about girlfriends, but only now and again. She doesn't want to think about her son and girlfriends, not yet. He doesn't need the fuss, not now, so soon, frying pan into the fire. He has his softness and his powerlifting, an unusual combination, sure, but only if you don't know Donny and this one astounding capability he has—his strength like Samson's. A couple of years ago she'd pushed him to find a coach, get training, she'd helped him phone around. Again, she takes the credit. It turned out that the coach, Carl—foul-mouthed, bull-necked Carl—made all the difference. Donny became a silver medallist the following summer.

Softness in a grown son is pleasant for a mother, in Kay's opinion. Softness connects back to when Donny was small. His smooth, soft legs and arms, she remembers, when he stood up in her lap and she held his cushiony knees, and laughed up at the pink colours in his round excited cheeks.

She knew of course, even as she held those fat legs, that nothing lasted, that soon he'd grow big as all babies do, and yet, as she sat there holding him, she remembers thinking that this moment somehow topped out her life: it was enough, it was plenty. After this she could rest, her work on earth was complete.

Well, the feeling passed quickly, as happens, yet, all these years on, how happy she still is right now that her big, gentle son called, she admits it to herself. She is very happy—overjoyed in fact, sitting here soaking up the filtered sunshine and thinking of him close by, giving her a ring...

She drains her coffee and switches on the radio for the local news, turns the knob along the dial in case there's a mention. A station breaks into 'Stuck On You'. She lets it play.

Pushing him away and yet pulling him back, Kay thinks, she can let this tension be. Helping him towards independence, but delighted about today, his thinking of her, sharing the glory. All day this joy will stay with her, she knows, even if he doesn't win. Whatever success he gets is in some measure hers, too.

She stands up, reaches for the still-wrapped newspaper, the coffee mug. Provided today isn't too busy she will carry out her plan, she is decided, grab an hour if she can to pop downtown to the arena, catch some of the action on the big screen outside. The previous four championships were all inter-state—Goulburn, Tamworth, even Cairns—impossible to get to without a few days' leave. But now the logic of rotation has brought the contest here. She hasn't arranged for a ticket, but all along she has hoped she might, without drawing attention, slip away from work and make a quick dash downtown.

Who would insist on keeping a distance? Rod, yes, certainly, but Rod has gone now. His turned-down mouth and withdrawn expression, all of that is over, in the past.

She reaches to the chair-back behind her, feels for the bulletproof jacket that in the office generally hangs there, and catches herself up short. She's not even dressed yet! Of course there's no jacket. She must hurry. The sun's much higher than she'd thought, needling her neck with hot fingers through the gaps in the trellis. It must be well past seven.

'Stuck On You' dwindles to buzzing. She switches the radio off, wasn't listening anyway, sticks the device under her arm, picks up the cup and the paper and elbows her way back into the house.

Putting everything down on the counter she starts dropping clothing as she goes, pyjama top, pyjama bottom, slippers, hairband. Then into the shower. Uniform. Shoes. And finally the bulletproof jacket. The effect of having the thing on is like getting into fancy dress. Every time, an instant transformation. See the person in the full-length mirror, in character, stern, dark, chiselled, defended. She thinks of Donny—perhaps at this very minute putting on his huge, reinforced powerlifting brace.

~

The first proper call comes into the duty office around one-thirty.

A woman's voice, musical but sharp-edged, panicky, 'My son...'

Kay pulls her notebook closer and makes wide eyes over at Aitch, her partner for the afternoon. Action at last, though, darn it, it could definitely have come an hour or so earlier...

Over morning coffee she had stupidly tempted fate by

checking the downtown traffic situation on her phone, had thought she was in the clear.

And now here she is, eating the cheese-and-tomato sandwich she brought from home more out of habit than hunger, letting herself think about the big screen outside at the arena, catching a glimpse of Donny in his belt, lifting some gigantic weight—is that how they do it, just lift it, without support, with muscle power alone?—and realising suddenly that the phone is ringing. Her brain must have gone scatty with too much coffee.

'My son's threatening me. Please, come quickly, soon as you can.'

'Thank you, we're here, we can hear you. Are you in immediate danger?'

'No, not immediate, but I feel threatened. My son...'

There is thudding in the background, then silence.

Kay hands the phone to Jake, the service officer at the front desk. Aitch has grabbed the car keys, taking them in one smooth curving movement from the hook while heading for the back, the car park. She reaches for her bulletproof jacket, snug on the back of her chair, and dashes at the sliding doors.

'I'll drive round, pick you up in front, Dunstan Terrace exit.'

The day has grown hot, easily over 40. The entrance is unshaded and the sweat bursts out across the back of her neck.

My son's threatening me, said that woman. *Come quickly*.

A son threatening a mother, can that be true?

Donny in his belt with his soft, conditioned hair, he'd not threaten a soul, would he, let alone his mother?

Oh, *men*, her own mother often sighs, as if that one word explained everything. Rod leaving without a word that spring morning, which is to say, three short SMSes. Donny's own father not paying a penny towards his upbringing, not even the music lessons he himself proposed, yet stockpiling gifts for other women in the laundry cupboard throughout their time together, cut-glass vases, tea sets, silk scarves—throughout their un-marriage, as her mother calls it.

Aitch pulls up, Kay reaches for the door handle and swings herself into the car.

It's not for her to stand around mulling the whys and wherefores, she tells herself sternly. It's for her to take action. She's on duty just the same as everyone else.

The house is down a narrow street lined with young mallee trees on both sides. A sky-blue front door stands open. At the back of the house, raised voices and a loud cawing sound. They ring the bell and then walk straight in, down the dark passage and to the back.

At first sight the tall boy in the back garden looks more confused than threatening. He is kicking the Hills Hoist post, flinging his long thin stem of a body around the small patch of lawn, his cheeks hot and indignant. A plume of hair flops over one side of his face, the other half of his head is shaved. His hands dangle like floppy spatulas by his side as he kicks. Everything about him from this angle looks soft, bendable, giving.

'Fuck,' he shouts over and over—it's the cawing, warbling noise. 'Fuck fuck fuck,' as if he's still getting used to saying the word, to speaking in a man's voice at all.

The mother is nowhere to be seen. The interior of the house is shadowy. Kay checks the name she keyed into her phone. Amy, the woman said, spelt like the French for loved, A-I-M-E-E, with that accent on the first e. You got that?

Kay begins to type *OK?* but at the same instant Aimée texts from somewhere inside the house.

Make yourself at home. Can't face him right now.

Kay calls her straight away. Aitch is just in front of her on the back doorstep, watching the boy. They hear Aimée's voice resonating somewhere.

'Be out as soon as I can,' she says. 'Can't stand to be near him right now, my son. In fact I can't even bear to look at him.'

Aitch and Kay step back into the house. They stand in the middle of the living room facing the big window out on to the garden, the boy in the centre of their view, his hair dark with sweat, his cheeks fiery. He's still kicking the post, but with diminishing fury. The long grass around the post has been trampled flat.

'Could murder a cup of tea right now,' says Aitch.

'Me too,' says Kay. She wishes vaguely he hadn't said murder.

She goes towards the fridge to check for milk but stops herself halfway. They shouldn't make themselves comfortable, not really, not without a proper invitation. She stays standing and Aitch stays standing. Their radio phones chatter at their belts—colleagues on other jobs, in other backyards.

Kay rests on one leg and looks at the photos stuck to the fridge with ladybird magnets, photos of the kicking boy at various younger ages, his arm around a dog, around a friend, around an older woman, probably a grandmother, blowing out the candles on a series of birthday cakes, his face each time grown broader. Kay counts five candles, six, eight, twelve.

'Isn't this weird?' Kay says. 'When I first walked in here I thought it could be my own place.'

'Previous life,' says Aitch.

'I mean it, Aitch, the shape of the garden and how the screen door fits alongside the picture window—it's the same. But not just the house. I have an exercise bike exactly like hers, also sat in the laundry, believe it or not. And then these photos on the fridge, just the same, in my case Donny through the ages—'

'Well, if it helps, Kay, you've never been here before. To my knowledge. You live on the other side of town.'

'Seriously, though, even that patch of white irises in the

garden, over there in the corner, I have the same irises. Even her tea is the same—see here, Ceylon.'

'Ladies of a certain age, Kay, with similar interests,' Aitch gives a cheeky grin that doesn't suit him. 'Maybe their houses end up looking alike.'

She decides to let it go. Aitch is like this, whatever the word is, straightforward or maybe tone-deaf—she's worked with him many times before.

'Even the bike colour is the same, Aitch,' she can't resist a last word. 'Same make *and* same colour. A parallel life more than previous life, I'd say.'

She biffs him lightly on the arm.

The biff makes him grunt involuntarily and the boy looks up, scowls at his reflection in the window. Then he suddenly frowns deeper and at the same moment they hear a noise at their backs. Aimée. Someone slight and dark is suddenly standing close behind them.

'So you've managed to make my son's acquaintance?'

The next instant the boy bursts into the house. Aitch and Kay spin around.

'Give me the phone.' He grabs at his mother's hand, wrings it to get the phone free. 'I want to talk to my dad. I want to tell him about this crazy woman. I don't want to live with her any more.'

Kay turns back fast enough to see Aimée squeeze her eyes tight shut.

'Come,' Aitch grabs the boy by the arm, 'Let's step outside again for a minute.'

'Get off, I know what I'm doing,' the boy shouts, but Aitch's clutch is firm.

'She's the mad one, the crazy one, not me,' he bellows over his shoulder, 'I don't want to be around her. She's not my mother any more. I hate her. I hate her so badly. She hates me, too.'

The woman is built like a girl—tiny waist, tiny wrists, everything else tiny, tiny thighs in kid's jeans, an ironed black shirt, tight-fitting and ruched around her ribcage, matte black hair, dyed, like Kay's own, tucked behind her ears.

She gestures to Kay to sit. Kay is suddenly aware of the bulletproof jacket tight around her own chest and stomach. She wishes she could take it off. She stays standing.

Through the picture window they see Aitch and the boy unstack two garden chairs and sit down at the wire-mesh table. See, another likeness, Aitch, Kay says to herself, a square wire-mesh table like the one on my porch.

The boy leans sideways in the chair, as far away from the police officer as possible. He is very young—fifteen, Kay thinks, not a day older. He projects a string of gob into the iris bed and Aitch rears forward, almost on top of him. Won't try that one again.

The mother, Aimée, chooses a straight-backed chair and turns it away from the window. When she moves she is like a trick of the light, a thin flash of darkness breaking up the sunlight in a forest.

'So young, my son, a month and ten days off his sixteenth birthday, would you believe it?' she says, as if reading Kay's thoughts. 'But not so young as to avoid threatening his mother. Just an hour ago he stood here on the step, towering over me, dragging at the screen door—look, the hinge is bent. I thought if he'd get it loose he could turn it on me. I was afraid.'

'Was there something that upset...?' Kay sits down.

'Who knows, I never know. Did I tell him to do his homework? Did I say I'd cut off his phone? I can't remember. All I know is, he's trying to get clear.'

'Clear?'

'He's trying to scour his way away from me. Scour it wide open. Like you might scour a pan.'

The boy dodges around Aitch, and pushes back through the screen door. Kay and the woman stand up in unison.

'You called the police out on me! This guy said. What mother calls the police? Let me speak to my dad.'

Aitch hands the boy his own phone. The boy stabs numbers into it. Almost immediately he begins to talk.

'She doesn't know what she's doing,' the boy caws into the phone. The three others stand staring at him. 'She's mad. She called the police. I need to get away. Please. I want to come and live with you.'

Aimée sits down and shrugs—a slight rise and fall of her shoulders. Her cheeks are shining, a skim of rainwater over stone. Kay can't bear to look at her. She moves in the direction of the fridge, those ladybird magnets.

'You hear what he says about me?' Aimée says quietly, addressing no one in particular. 'Repeating the things he's heard from his father. What can I do? When he began damaging my door, my house, I felt desperate. All I could think was, call for help.'

In mid-sentence the boy stops shouting into the phone. Aitch leads him outside, still flinging his arms. The screen door bangs behind them.

Kay and the woman sit and watch the boy pacing the yard, Aitch leaning against the hoist.

'You can leave and go somewhere for a while,' Kay says quietly. 'You don't have to stay here. You can go to a friend till it blows over.'

'But it's my home. I need to be here. My things are here. I don't want to leave him with my things. He shouldn't be able to oust me.'

'Still, to use your words, you also wouldn't want to oust him?'

'How could I? He's my son, whatever he says. Could I

put him out on the street? No. I don't want him to get into trouble. You have that phone number for families. I just wanted someone to come along, be here, see for themselves.'

'You can call our number at any time,' Kay says.

She almost wants to add, I also have a son, but she doesn't. She wouldn't know how to go on. She couldn't then say, *Oh, men*, like her mother, or, *boys will be—*, or, I do so totally see where you're coming from. Between the two young men, there's no ground for comparison.

She catches Aitch's eye through the window, points her head in the direction of the door. Aitch knows what she means. If she's to have any time at the arena, they should be heading on.

~

The top name on the big screen in the arena car park is not Donny's. For a moment Kay's not sure what disappoints her more—his name not being up there or the notice that it's all over, she's missed the prize-giving, she won't see him compete at all.

But then, looking again, it does say *Donny*. She twigs what she's reading. His name is up there anyway. He has won *something*, looks like another silver medal. Well I never, she tells herself, locking the car, there you go, not bad, son, not bad.

Reeking of sweat, Donny towers over her in the arena foyer. If he were to hug her without bending, his arms would meet around her crown. They could crush her skull like a nut, she thinks. And she, Kay, is not short, she is not tiny Aimée. She steps suddenly away.

They move into the arena club-room buffeted by large powerlifters and their families. Massive men pump Donny's arm. Round tables are laid with white cloths, white crockery, pale orchid centrepieces. The food on the buffet is also mainly pale—pale and glutinous—white-fish mousse, cold chicken, potato salad, coleslaw.

Donny is ravenous. He piles a plate high. Kay also piles her plate, knowing he will eat most of it, too, 'just a smidgen, Mum,' creep his fork across and pick up titbits as he did as a child.

Cramming the white food into his mouth, Donny tells her three times over about his near-winning lift. And *then*, he says, and *then*, with each *then* hitting the table with his fist. She understands why he's putting the emphasis. If you hadn't quite made gold, you'd want to give your back a pat.

Still, he's very loud. His blaring reminds her of that young boy earlier, in the backyard, what was his name? Aimée's son? She can't believe she doesn't remember. Did she catch his name? It was Aitch who spoke to him.

Kay looks around the tables. Large groups surround the other powerlifters. She and Donny are just two to their table. Everyone around seems to be telling versions of his story. She's hearing the same names, the same lines. Donny has been a star, though not the biggest star. The winner is someone with a Croatian name. She can't bear to ask Donny who it is. The beating noise of his fist is stubbing out her concentration. And then I lifted it, *then*, he says again, hitting his fist. Their coffee cups rattle.

She feels for her bulletproof jacket but, no, it's back in the car. She'd like to have it here with her now, have it on. Donny's fist beating the table is making her feel irritated, queasy—either that or the seafood mousse. Donny keeps turning to her and half-winking, half-grimacing, as though he's pointing to some secret they alone share.

She wants to step back, peel away this closeness he's folding around her, this sticky mix of intimacy and boasting. This is no way to be with your mother, can't he see? so sickly close and soft. It's definitely no way to be here, in this public place. After a win like his, he should be grappling his mates to his chest, or his girlfriend, his wife, not his mother.

They finish their coffee and Donny leads the way out on to the balcony. The balcony runs the length of the club-room. It is dark out here, quiet and cool. A few small groups stand talking. The hazy sky is empty of stars and a laser light in the direction of Elizabeth Square strokes the low clouds.

Kay checks her phone. Almost she hoped there might be a message, that she might be recalled to that same house, Aimée's—check she's doing OK. But the screen shows no new activity. Donny begins winking again, winking and lifting one shoulder, and now she sees why. The gold-medal winner's huge back looms over the next group along. Donny means to point at him. The winner has the trophy in his arms.

Might they go over? she gestures.

She still wonders what exactly a powerlifter *does*, especially to win? Despite all Donny has said. She'd like to ask the winner.

In answer Donny clasps her arms and pins them to her sides, an old trick. So she can't put out her hand, say hello. So her attention is all his.

Wriggle out. She wants to make herself small and slip out of his grip. His hands feel sticky. They cling. She wants to prise his insistent hands off her skin.

She turns away and faces out across the cricket ground, watches the laser beam reaching and stretching. She is a good step away but still senses Donny's closeness, the damp heat radiating from him. She remembers the joy she felt this morning, looking forward, hoping to catch sight of her son. What was all that about, that elation? If she once knew, she doesn't now.

Donny leans his arms on the balcony rail and lets his head hang down. He looks dog-tired. He has at last fallen silent, a small mercy. Her queasiness has gone. His noise must have brought it on, not the mousse. Before, before today, she would have reached out to him at this moment, rubbed his back. But now she doesn't. She does nothing and she says nothing. She can't think of a thing to say.

Something about today has brought this change, Kay thinks, but what it is eludes her. Even as she and Aitch closed the sky-blue door of Aimée's house behind them and left the boy cawing in the backyard and his mother sitting tiny and dark on the straight-backed chair with her back to the light, it escaped her. At some point today she learned something she didn't see when she sat out on the porch this morning, but it's obscure to her now. It's left behind in the shadows of that house that's the very spit of her own. It's there somewhere in the squeezed-shut eyes of that tiny woman in black. It's somewhere in the photos of the hugging boy stuck on the fridge with ladybird magnets, in the spaces between the candles, in the shadows leaping on the walls.

Supermarket Love

WHEN I WALK by the security-office door on my break and it's open, I try to snatch a look. The supermarket security guards keep the door open when it's hot, over forty. Right now, mid-February, that's most of the time.

'You must get boiling with that headscarf on,' my friend Skye says, almost whispering. We've been friends for weeks before she says this. I've seen the other girls wear strappy tops under their brown supermarket overalls.

It's only us in the staff tearoom, me and Skye in the plastic chairs, Mo standing against the wall in his silver trainers, drinking Nescafé. Mo glances up, he doesn't miss a thing.

I look at him, I look at Skye.

'It's not as bad as you think,' I say. 'The air-conditioning helps. I never get cold.'

'That's what my mother says,' Mo murmurs.

Columns of black-and-white CCTV screens cover the security-office walls. There are no windows, the same as in the staff tearoom.

What can the security guards see on their screens? What can't they see? This is what I want to find out. This is why I peek. But usually I don't get more than a few seconds. The screens all look the same, the aisles all look the same. The security guards sit with their feet up on the desks drinking cold Pepsi.

Plus right now they have giant red Valentine's Day cardboard hearts hanging in the aisles, blocking the view.

Defeats their purpose, you might say.

Gives ideas, my mother might say.

More ways than one, I think to myself.

Already I know the place I'm looking for won't be the frozen-goods aisle, its corridor of smooth fridge-doors. Nowhere to hide there, and freezing cold, too.

It also won't be the open-plan sweets area with the help-yourself display units, the imported Valentine's Day chocolates in stacks of red and pink. Everything in the sweets area is waist-high. The supermarket expects sweets and chocolates to go, also grapes, cherries, cherry tomatoes—anything that's finger food. Mo says so. Some days we set out sample trays of cherry tomatoes. They all go in twenty.

Everyone does it, Mo says. He's worked here for longer than us girls have. He's been in this country for longer, too. Stuff just walks into people's mouths, he says—smarties, plain old marshmallows, jelly-babies, everyone thinks they can sample one or two without anyone noticing. Maybe no one does. The security guards wait for bigger prey.

My heart jumps. It jumps the minute he says, you won't believe how much just walks. Mo, I see, is *also* taking looks at the screens. Mo is *also* wondering about places out of sight.

But then, who wouldn't want to find a hidden place some-where to break up their day? Who wouldn't take a moment to skate, slide, twirl a trolley? Skye once turned a somersault. It was quiet, close to closing. She did it in a second, flick flack, just like that.

Mo knows more, though. He has the lowdown. The shoppers picking their noses in empty aisles, plucking at their underwear, squeezing the fresh bread till it's nearly flat—Mo knows their secrets, he has it all cased out. When he tells me about something he has spotted I blush. I let my headscarf fall lower over my cheeks to hide my blushes. But I come back to him.

'By the bleach, I think,' I tell Mo. 'That's the best place.'

See if he agrees. From what I can tell, people don't pause and browse in the cleaning-products aisle. Any security guard with knowhow won't waste time watching those screens. Shoppers go straight to the place on the shelf. They don't linger, they don't steal bleach. Unless.

'Uh-huh, Farhana, so now we know. Bleach section. We know where to find you when next you have something to hide.'

And he winks at me. My heart jolts.

The first time we spoke my heart did the same jolt, a skip out of time. It was in the staffroom. The fan was on, another hot day. He caught my eye and without pausing said *salaam alaikum* in proper Australian from behind his Pepsi can.

'*Salaam alaikum*,' I said, straight away dropping my eyes, but not before my heart turned around and I returned his look, may God forgive me. And then added, 'Hello.'

We've kept it to Hello ever since, but my heart still jolts.

It's all crazy. It should be stopped.

~

Dear Veronica, I'd write, if I had the courage. *Dear Veronica* or *Pamela* or *Monica*—these names that no women I meet ever have.

I love him. He is...he is... When I hear his voice in the next aisle my breathing goes insane.

Dear Monica, Dear Pamela, I'm on the verge of writing. Can't talk to my mum, can't talk to my aunt, though she's younger with highlights under her headscarf. Can't talk to anyone at school. They'd want to go *huh*, is that for real? Hide their real feelings with a cough. Like Skye. 'You serious?' she says. 'You feel bad just looking a boy in the eye?'

So all I can think of is an agony auntie like you, *Dear Veronica*, from Mum's *Woman* magazine. There are rows and rows of magazines like yours here in the shop by the checkouts. I restack them every day.

The best way of getting to know this country, Mum says. What the men think is on TV. What the women think is in these magazines.

But what she reads in the magazines gives her worries, the agony columns especially. Reading the columns, she heaves low grieving sighs and calls my aunt. They talk about the nice Afghan boy up in Brisbane, our cousin five or twenty-five times removed. They talk about nice Afghan boys in other cities around the world. This country is too full of temptation and false allure, my mother tells my aunt, not in English. We need to move fast to get her settled.

Dear Veronica, Dear Pamela, I'd like to write if I could, if I had courage, if I didn't think Mum would read the letter and find me out in a flash.

I work with him and can't stop thinking about him, I want to write. *Whenever we're stacking shelves I want to reach across, I want to hold his hand. I think it will be a warm dry hand. I want to be his girlfriend but I have no idea. Can I say girlfriend? I don't know what girlfriend means.*

I wouldn't know how to begin.

Would they even understand? Everything dear Monica, Pamela, Veronica say is about promise and possibility, grabbing promise, widening possibility, having it all. Isn't this the land of big flat horizons and big possibilities? Isn't this the twenty-first century? Isn't this the place and the time where you take your opportunities in both hands?

But that's why I'm writing, I'd say. But wouldn't say, can't say. *Take my opportunities*, what does that mean? What is that *my*? What is that *take*?

See, the place where I'm from, that place—you can hardly say the word, because people look at you, the name of the landlocked country with deep caves and valleys up in the clouds where outsiders get killed and insiders get killed, the place that was once the hub of the world, everything trading in every direction east to west and south to north from the time of Alexander, walnuts, silks, carpets, upholstered chairs, mulberry saplings, silverware, glass goblets, masked goshawks, falcons... There, in that place, what your family wants goes. Families depend on a girl not choosing for herself.

Opposite of home, this new country, Mum often says. You walk to any edge of this country and you fall into the sea. You don't walk *on*.

Why walk to the edge at all? says my aunt, when millions of people are walking to the edges of their countries trying to get to this one. Drowning in small boats.

Only reason we got here, Mum says, your father's a damn good doctor, and we're a good family, and you and your sister are good girls, *good as gold*. That bit she says in English. *Good as gold*.

Dear Veronica, I want to write, *Dear Pamela*, I think I know Mo likes me because when we're stacking together he tells me about himself. He tells me about growing up in Victor Harbour, the only Lebanese family in town, the only Muslim family, his father the caretaker of the caravan park. He tells me they had a butcher shop once, but the town wasn't big enough for a halaal butchery. He tells me his mother stays at home. She stays at home all the time. Mo's father walked him to school.

Dear Monica, I want to write, I think I know Mo likes me because he tells me private things about himself. He tells me about the Airfix planes he used to build as a kid. American Airforce planes mainly—Mustangs, Harrier jets. To this day his mother has them dangling from the ceiling in their living room. He's embarrassed saying this but he shouldn't be. I like that he built Airfix planes. I like to know everything about him.

He tells me his first job was in a tablet repairs shop that also sold XL and XXL clothes on the side. The shop for the guys who get fat playing games all day on their tablets, Mo said, and made me laugh. Who am I to talk, though? he went on. Spend about four hours every day on the Xbox.

When instead we could be walking up and down the Parade together chatting, I silently say to him. When we could be sitting together in the shade of the bandstand on Memorial Square drinking smoothies.

Dear Veronica, I want to write, I think I know Mo likes me because he tells me about stuff he reads on the internet. Did you know trees are sociable? he tells me. I mean, within their different species? Their roots reach out to each other. That's why the giant sequoias never grow tall away from the big forests of America. They grow tallest together, reaching out.

I think, *reaching out*, what is he telling me? And I say, it's different for us then. We leave our countries to grow tall elsewhere, over the sea.

In reply he just looks at me. And I remember Victor Harbour. I remember the halaal butchery and the caravan park. I remember he has lived here ages, unlike me.

Dear Pamela, I want to write, I think I know he likes me because when I'm working on an aisle refilling shelves, he makes sure that when he places boxes of new products on the top shelf they jut out a bit, so that even a short person like me can reach them. So that I can stretch up, wiggle them out and then pull them down.

Dear Monica, I also want to write, I think I know for sure he likes me because today, the day before Valentine's Day, he asked me to help him stack in the cleaning-products area. He remembered what I'd told him and he made a date, almost.

He leaned right over and said smiling, 'At least with the headscarf the camera won't see you blush.'

And I said, don't know where the words came from, I said, 'It won't show anyway, the screens are black and white.'

So today, Veronica, we have a game plan of sorts. Am I saying *we*? I don't know what *we* means, I do know what *we* means. Well, we, he and I, for the first time we have a plan.

Of course we've walked our way towards each other down all kinds of aisles, crossing paths between the washing-powder towers, the jams and chutneys and *just add milk* pale-pink instant puddings. But then I tell him about safety in bleach and he asks me for help.

We move down the cleaning-products aisle from opposite directions just as normal except today all this is planned. We are sidestepping like dancers, even our stacking hands are moving in sync. My heart goes mad.

I see his silver trainers out of the corner of my eye. I see the red cardboard love-hearts hanging from the ceiling, even here in cleaning products. I see the red, foil-wrapped chocolate mini-heart he is holding in his hand. At this time of year there are mini-hearts piled in plastic bowls at the checkout at $1 each. I refill the bowls every few hours so they always look full.

He puts the chocolate in my hand. It is soft from lying in

his palm. We reach the opposite ends of the aisle and change direction, we cross paths a second time. He tucks a second chocolate into my hand. He moves off, thinks better of it, does a funny moonwalk turn and pulls a third chocolate out of his pocket. I laugh. This chocolate is even warmer to touch. It is going squishy inside its foil.

He offers to peel it for me. I shake my head. I can't bear to close my hand over the softening chocolate, the three squishy chocolate hearts.

What do the cameras see? What do the screens in the security office show? A boy shelf-packer and a girl shelf-packer working together, just that, though, wait a minute, their crossing point is always closer to *his* end of the aisle, may God forgive her. That means she sidles faster, she wants to go quicker. She is ahead of him, ahead of herself.

On the day before Valentine's Day I collect three chocolates from Mo's hand in cleaning products.

The next day, Valentine's Day itself, we play our sidestepping game again and I collect four.

I put my hearts in a paper bag and hang it on my hook in the staffroom. Then I worry about the chocolate melting and I go to store the bag in the fridge where we keep the milk for our coffee.

And then, *Dear Veronica*, I see Skye has also received a chocolate heart. She has left her heart on a shelf in the fridge marked with her name on a post-it. Skye's chocolate heart is not the mini kind. It is one of the $7.95 hearts that we sell in sweets, the type that guys in suits rushed in to buy today at lunchtime along with bunches of cellophane-wrapped red and pink carnations, hoping to make up later for what they forgot to give this morning. My job today is to spritz the flowers on the hour with cool water to keep them sprightly in the heat.

Dear Pamela, I want to write, I don't want to write, I think I don't know anything, I think I do know something. I think Mo has given Skye this $7.95 chocolate heart.

I remember how in these last few days of hot weather Mo has gone outside during our breaks to stand in the shade by the back exit and chat to the shelf-packers who smoke. Skye is a smoker.

'It's the sociability,' he says passing me on his way out. 'Humans like sociability like trees do,' I think I hear him say.

The smokers stand in the shade of the Queensland box by the exit and kick the fallen tree-fruit and exhale their smoke up into the branches. I see them through the crack in the fire doors. Skye stands against the box trunk with her overall poppers open to show her strappy top underneath and squints into the smoke rising from her cigarette.

Skye knows what girlfriend means. Of course she does. She knows what girlfriends do. They squint through their lashes and blow smoke into boys' faces. What Lebanese boy from Victor Harbour wouldn't want to stand with a girl like Skye in the cool shade and give her chocolate hearts on Valentine's Day and see her screw up her eyes at him?

At the end of the day Skye has six chocolate hearts in the fridge, two big, four small.

Dear Monica, I want to write, all I know is, Mo couldn't have given her *all* of those chocolates.

~

It is over forty-five degrees today, even hotter than it was on Valentine's Day. First thing this morning we took down the red cardboard hearts hanging in the aisles. The boxes of chocolates are two for the price of one and probably melting and turning white underneath their foil. The door of the CCTV room is wide open. The security guards have got used to me standing in the doorway. They don't look round when I pause to take a look.

Mo is visible to me all around the supermarket. His bright silver trainers show up white on the screens. Since Valentine's Day I try not to go where he goes. I avoid his plans.

The fact is I've been punished. The eye of God sees everything and I went too fast. I was giddy. Sidling sideways down the aisles to meet with a boy I hardly know and receive warm chocolates from his warm hand, it meant too much.

Skye and Mo meantime pretend nothing is going on. He joins her and the other smokers under the box tree. They take plastic cups of Nescafé from the machine in the staffroom. I see him hand out cigarettes. He carries a box in his pocket even though he doesn't smoke, or not that I can see. I see him offer to light her cigarette with one of the orange plastic lighters we sell at the checkout. I see her flick her hair and giggle into his face.

At the end of the break he offers her gum and she takes it. Freshen her smoky breath. Back in the staffroom he offers me gum too, smiling as though nothing is wrong. I say no, really quick.

I find a new favourite place to stack, at the shelves of hair products. This spot is directly under the eye of one of the cameras. I know this from my CCTV peeking. I like how smoothly the tall bottles of shampoo and conditioner and hair serum stack. I like how they shine like candy—green, pink, raspberry and orange—and I like how they smell of almonds and honey. I go back often to neaten the rows. I like to think no customer could ever guess how many times the display has been touched, lined up, straightened. I want them to think they are the very first today to reach out their hand and select just this shiny shampoo.

And then he is suddenly stacking here beside me. *Salaam alaikum*, he says, same as that first time.

Dear Monica, I'd write if I was still thinking of writing, *Dear Pamela*, his hands are moving in rhythm with mine.

Dear Veronica, I won't let myself think but still I think it, he has sought me out.

I slow my stacking hands and he goes slower, to my tempo. I look up at the CCTV to remind him it's there, our supermarket eye. He looks up too, then back at me. That loose shrugging of his shoulders under his shirt. I start to blush.

Dear Veronica, I see our hands playing in harmony over the *full and luscious* fortifying serums, and the *pure shine* conditioners and gels, and though my headscarf shields my cheek I know he can see my blush without even looking, and I know that he knows what I am thinking.

This is what I am thinking, what I am trying not to think. I think that by leaning in his direction just a fraction I can let the weight of my hair under my headscarf brush against his arm. So he can feel the touch of what only the eye of God and my mother and the mirror at night can see.

Dear Pamela, I want to write, this boy at work, the one I liked, I don't know what to do about him. He follows me around, he watches the cameras just like I do, he always knows where to find me. I no longer trust him. I mean, I don't trust myself around him.

When I'm around him I lose my senses. Even when I see him on screen I lose my bearings. When I see him light Skye's cigarette or straighten her collar after she's refastened her poppers or, once, curl her hair back around her ear, and then when he comes over to stack shelves with me as though nothing was the matter, I can't help myself. I think warm chocolate hearts. I think finger food, cherries, cherry tomatoes, orange plastic cigarette lighters.

I also think of hairgrips with pearly tips, the kind I use to fasten my headscarf. He offered me a new packet today when we finished stacking and straightening the shampoos.

It won't help, *Dear Monica*, to advise me to get his number and invite him to a movie like you do with everyone else. It's gone beyond that point.

I go to stand in the doorway of the CCTV room till the two security guys notice me. I don't have to say anything, I only point. I point to Mo in his bright trainers moving across the screens. I point to his quick Airfixing fingers flying here and there, all over the place. See his fingers reaching for stuff, I say, just small stuff, true, chewing gum, cigarettes, lighters, matches, hand creams, hairgrips with pearly tips, coloured elastic bands, stuff that girls like. But doesn't it all stack up? See how it fills his pockets to overflowing.

'We'll observe things for a while and then take steps,' the head security guard says. 'The manager will be grateful. You've been very quick to see this.'

'I always did stack quicker than him,' I say, and close my fingers round the unopened packet of pearly hairgrips in my overalls pocket.

Synthetic Orange

ONE WARM EVENING that late summer, my boyfriend Gregor clasped a new bracelet on to my wrist. At the exact same moment the waiter placed two steaming plates on our table under the stars. We had chosen the same dish, langoustines in a salsa de jugo on a bed of linguine, the chef's special.

Waving at the steam, I admired my newly adorned wrist.

You like message-type things, he said. That's what I thought when I saw it.

We were staying in a small Spanish beach resort without special features, two big hotels, a few bars and a tourist-village complex built onto a narrow strip of grey sand beside the Gran Via Mediterranea.

The same sea no matter your entry-point, we had said to each other the day we booked. Same sea, same waves, same temperatures. The makings of a good holiday. No matter about the strip development, the mean grey sand. I was there for the swimming. He was there to be there. For much of the time so far we had got on. I knew this was why I had earned the gift.

It's for a charity, Gregor added, looking cunning. Or maybe he was scrunching up his eyes at the flag of steam coming up from the pasta. You pay a lot more than the worth of it.

I noticed yet again his bony hands, the thinness and paleness of his fingers. I never caught sight of them without being surprised. Their delicacy, fineness. When his character wasn't what you'd call fine. Not bad, just not fine. Even the lines on his palms were straight and fine, without loops.

The bracelet was orange in colour, a tooled leather hoop fastened with a silver magnetic clip, fashioned by a designer called Olaf or Thor, something Scandinavian. It came with an accompanying leaflet. Gregor now smoothed out the leaflet, the text facing him.

He'd got the bracelet the night before at the exhibition we were both meant to be at. A friend of the artist Zozo had pressed the invitation into our hands at the Irish Harp Bar. They were worried about being low on numbers, she fussed. But I had caught the sun, so it was a good opportunity for an early night. Gregor hated early nights. He liked to have something on in the evenings. He needed some promise that the day was never completely over.

Zozo the artist made neon-lit portraits of her friends and acquaintances, said the blurb on the invitation. The pictures were embellished with appliqué devices, the cut-off bottoms of margarine tubs and yoghurt cartons painted over in oils and pasted with passport photographs of the painting's subject.

Better than you might have thought, Gregor said, reporting back late last night, waking me up to tell me. More colourful, he said, more moving. But still I found myself spending most of my time at Olaf's bracelet stand at the exit.

Olaf, it seemed, was another friend of Zozo's we might have met in the Irish Harp.

I ran my finger along the loop of the bracelet. The outside was lined with a synthetic orange material.

It's that waterproof stuff, you know, that the rescue jackets are made of. Gregor tapped the leaflet. It bothered me his tapping finger was moving so delicately, even languidly, that his bones were so very thin and fine. You know, he said, the jackets those migrants coming over in boats get given when they're rescued.

I know, I said.

Live migrants, he added. Obviously. They came off live migrants. Olaf picks the jackets of the ones who come out live, dump the jackets on the beach as soon as they get to the shore.

Seconds later, after a mouthful of linguine, Gregor repeated this fact. I did make sure, he said, live migrants, as if I hadn't been concentrating the first time.

I unhooked the bracelet, to get the feel of the clasp, then put it on again. The metallic fastener made a satisfying clinking sound as it closed and the memories rushed in. At the exact moment it clipped back on, the memories began to flow through me like a waking dream, scenes of flow and flood and ebb, a tide of memory so strong I had to get up from the table with my linguine untouched.

You feeling sick again? Gregor followed me to the edge of the restaurant patio.

I unclasped the bracelet and the images receded. I clasped it on again and the tide flooded back. I followed him back to the table as though nothing had happened, the bracelet in my hand.

It's very special, I told Gregor, but I do like to wear colours that match. You know that.

That evening I had my loose blue dress on.

Later, I went on to the roof of our holiday flats to smoke a cigarette. Usually I say I have given up smoking but tonight was an exception. A huge orange moon just beyond its term hung like an omen in the sky.

I took the bracelet out of my dress pocket and fastened it around my wrist. The clip clinked shut and in the same instant the memories crashed over me like a breaking wave.

~

I remembered my first swim of the holiday, off our grey beach, a night-time swim under a pitch-black sky. I struck out into the inky dark waters and instantly lost my bearings, unusual for me. I often swim after dusk, always without mishap, but that night a week ago the water was choppy. Suddenly I noticed that the street lights on the Gran Via were beginning to sweep past at speed, or I past them, as if I were caught in a moving train.

I had put the memory out of my mind, yet here it was, the warm dark waters splashing against my shoulders, stirring, restless and pushing, the scatter of tiny droplets the wind combed off the top of the waves, their lightness mocking the force of the rollers dragging me along. Not under. I didn't want to think *under*.

I remembered the long black shadows cast on the beach by the shore lights, and then the instant when the push of the tide on my legs became a pull, not the rhythm of the waves, steady, lulling, but something more insistent, something about *under*.

Then I was somewhere else, several metres down from where I had entered the water, the current half spinning me, and, suddenly again, I was past the headland at the end of the beach, and a submerged rock grazed my knee. I had not expected rocks, not this far out.

I could see the reflected street lights dancing over the surface of the water. I definitely couldn't see under. I couldn't see anyone on shore. There was no one to raise an alarm.

Did I think of Gregor? Not straight away. I don't like to watch you swim, he always said, I'm not your parent. He would be somewhere on the street beyond, on a bench, head down, chin uplit, checking his phone, his thin fingers wandering spider-like over the screen.

There was just the current and me inside it, not quite under, definitely not yet under.

I struck out in the direction of the next beach, beyond the headland. A wave slapped me full in the face. I swallowed water, told myself not to cough. Another wave struck my ear so hard it rang. Then, striking out again, I felt hard sand under my feet.

I walked back to the first beach by way of the road, panting hard, my hair dripping down my back.

That was a short swim, said Gregor, looking up from his phone as I approached. For you. I thought you'd be gone ages.

It was lovely out, I said. There was a strong current. I had to swim quite hard.

~

The toddler I looked after two years back, a boy, his name gone from my memory. Up on the roof I remembered him, too. On holiday that year with my mother, in a beach apartment a lot like ours, the toddler and his parents in the neighbouring flat. The parents paid well for time in the afternoons to catch some siesta.

The boy and I were in the waves, paddling hand in hand. I used his bucket to catch up water and toss it out to sea. He liked the sparkles the droplets made and clapped his hands to see them, each time pulling away from me just an instant.

The wave came from nowhere. One second he was standing there in his blue-and-yellow-striped swimming shorts, clapping his hands. The next second I couldn't see him and the milky wave was swirling around my thighs.

I threw myself flat into the water in the space where he had stood. I felt the rushing sliding sand the wave had unsettled. Nothing else.

I threw myself down again. Coming up that second time I saw a fragment of his blue-and-yellow striped shorts further down the beach balloon and disappear again. As I ran in their direction, the wave pulled back and he was suddenly in front of me, face down in the water, naked, his hands clawing the sand. I dragged him up, turned him round, and saw his eyes were open, his nose and mouth full of sand.

Sunbathers swarmed towards us. A woman took the child from me and laid him on his back on the beach, away from the water.

Doctor, she said over and over, Doctor. She put her hands on his chest, and her lips over his mouth.

Quickly she came up again.

Is OK, she said. Is lucky, is very lucky.

The child looked up at the sky, and made no noise. I sat beside him, and put my hand on his warm fat thigh.

Is your baby? she asked.

The wave came from nowhere, I gasped at her. Nowhere.

Nowhere, she agreed. It came from nowhere. He came back from nowhere.

I bundled the naked child in his towel, and took him back to the flats. If his parents had been there then, I would have told them everything. But they had gone to catch a cold beer at a café on the beach front. A note in black felt-tip was stuck on the fridge.

I dressed the child and wrapped him up tightly in a fresh towel. I don't know why I wrapped him. For a while we sat together quietly on the edge of his bed.

All right? I asked him several times. All right? He nodded silently but I couldn't be sure, not when thin streams of yellow liquid came from his ears, running down his neck, soaking the hem of the towel.

Later we sat and drew patterns on my legs with the black felt-tip till his parents returned.

They had enjoyed more than one cold beer and paid me extra for my time.

I gave back the extra, told them it was no trouble. I also said I was sorry but when I was changing the child on the beach, I'd left his swimming trunks behind by mistake.

Then I pointed out the weekend was coming up.

And so it is, the toddler's father said pleasantly. Till Monday, then, LeeAnn. Sadly, as we told your mother, Monday will be the last day of our holiday.

The child raised his hand and said a sing-song goodbye. Bye-bye LeeAnn. Bye-bye. Bye-bye.

I did not babysit the toddler again. There was a heatwave that Monday and the family decided to stay in. The father popped round before breakfast. He said they hoped they'd see us again next year. It had been a perfect holiday.

I asked him to give my love to the child.

Love back, said the father. You two had such times together. By way of answer I showed him the child's loopy black drawings still marked on my legs.

~

Up on the roof smoking, dragging warm clouds of smoke into my lungs, I also remembered Esme my school friend, Esme whom the river didn't at first give back. A few months before our final exams Esme walked into the river that runs through our town and past her house, the same brown fast-moving river we'd watched on wet days from her living room when we were smaller. She had always kept her eye on it, even when we were playing, that huge silent river flowing by pocked with rain, sending its silver feelers across the road towards the houses.

Will the river ever come into the house? Esme would often ask her mother.

They'll bring us sandbags before it comes, her mother said back, every time.

But I saw her pluck the long, brown slugs off the walls and the curtains and throw them outside while pretending to tidy. And each time she gave Esme a look, to check if she had noticed.

At Esme's funeral three months later they said she had gone to where she was happy. I wondered how they could be sure. She'd left her coat behind, they said, folded neatly on top of her shoes standing side by side on the river bank, and a notebook open on a line of poetry she had copied out spread on top of that. Her dad held the notebook in unsteady hands. *The river is a strong brown god*. Rain had blotted some of the words.

She went in to see how it felt, I thought, the strong brown god. It was just as likely. She went to check the strength of the current, to test how fast it could push her along. Standing there in my pew at the back of the church, I imagined her floating spread-eagled, lying like a star on the rippling water. She went in to feel what it was like to float on a river in spate, I thought. She wanted to see the orange glimmers in the misty night sky reflected in the water, writhing like phosphorescent snakes. She wanted to know how far she could go, how far the water would propel her.

I knew how far. We all now knew. She went beyond the footbridge and the marina for small boats and our secret diving place where the smaller river joined the bigger and the reed beds just beyond that where the frogs spawned, and then the concrete wharf at the edge of the pub before the lock—the concrete wharf with the iron hoops at a reachable distance that she was aiming to grab, just in time, as we did every summer, with a quick upwards clasp, to pull herself out.

I thought it just as likely that she had gone out for a float. I was sure it was just as likely that she hoped to be back before long.

~

And then I remembered swimming out in the bay earlier today, far out, where it's no longer possible to see the bottom, and thunk, my arm hit a bag of rubbish dropped off some yacht. I raised my head and saw in front of my nose something like a limb, grey-green, lumpy beneath the saturated and now translucent skin. I threw my arms back in shock and heard another swimmer come up on a bodyboard beside me.

Vale vale? he said, and then, in English, OK?

He reached out and dragged the bag on to his board. At the same moment a shoal of small silver fishes leapt over his arm.

Mounted on his board, the bag still looked like a drowned limb.

No worry, is not what we think, he said, and paddled on.

~

By now I had smoked two cigarettes up there on the roof under the orange moon and my head ached with tiredness. I unclasped the bracelet and at the same instant the memories running through me drained away. Downstairs I took the second dose of the morning-after pill I had picked up at lunchtime from the English-speaking GP. Better safe than sorry. Olaf's leaflet about helping refugees with his bracelets had folded itself around the box of pills in my bag.

Gregor was lying on his back on the settee.

Gregor, I said, it's over. We are over.

What was that? he asked, and tossed his head to the side.

He flicked his fringe in just that way when he came up out of the waves after a swim.

You feeling OK? he said after a pause. It must have been the twentieth time that holiday.

Yes, I'm OK, I said. I'm just saying we should split up.

But we have that parachute ride booked, he said, as if putting a question to the light fitting. Tomorrow. Why don't we stay together at least for that?

~

High up over the wrinkled sea the next day, the parachute gondola swayed us back and forth. Gregor held my left hand in his smooth, thin-boned right. Far ahead was the motorboat dragging the parachute cord. The boat painted a white arrow on the dark-blue water.

From the gondola, the umbrellas and bathers on the grey beach looked bigger than I had imagined. And the Gran Via and the whitewashed beach resorts beyond ours further away. The long shore and the wide sea didn't give perspective. Below, there were one or two small vessels, floating as if airborne on the water, and a boat drawn up on a neighbouring beach, painted blue and white, and a white cruise liner far out to sea.

Quietly I pulled the bracelet from my shorts pocket and clipped it on. Till now I hadn't dared. Then I looked straight down beneath us at the beach where we swam, at that small boat close to shore, just the one small boat moving in the waves.

The people in the boat looked dark against the glistening water. They were wearing bright-orange rescue jackets but the rest of them was dark. The dense afternoon light sparkled around their reaching arms.

I leaned forward to see better. I saw one of the people in the boat jump out. I saw him lose his footing, flounder, then right himself. I saw other people on board crowd forwards. Alone, the man began to drag the boat up the beach. One metre, two. Then others jumped out to help him. There were three or four dark figures in orange silhouetted against the diamond-bright water. The sunbathers lay on their towels with their eyes closed.

Look, I said, that boat!

What boat? said Gregor, following the direction of my pointing. I can't see a boat.

That boat, I said again, pointing with my bracelet-encircled arm. Those people.

Gregor looked. He peered. He did try to peer.

It's the people trying to make it across, I said. Look, they've nearly made it.

Gregor looked again, straining forwards. The gondola rocked.

Look, I said again, they're running across the beach.

I can't see a thing, Gregor said.

I unclipped the bracelet. When he quit looking I put it back in my pocket.

The motorboat took a looping turn and our gondola swayed some more. I let go his hand. The wind began booming in the parachute.

Next time a friend of yours goes night-swimming, I said to Gregor, shouting over the noise, Keep a look-out. People who go out to sea usually aim to come back.

Of course they do, said Gregor. When did I ever say otherwise?

He pushed his weight against the back of the gondola, so that it tipped nearly upside down and we were pitched face forwards, our straps pulling us back. The sea spread out above us like the sky.

So, he asked, turning directly to me, are you going to give me a second chance?

A drowning person doesn't get a second chance, I said.

~

The minute we touched down at Gatwick I said I'd walk by myself into the airport building. I hadn't returned to the subject of breaking up, but I still wanted to walk by myself.

Whatever you want, Gregor said sullenly.

Drinking usually made him sullen. In the departure lounge he had treated himself to a summer *oferta*: two pink gins for the price of one. And then two more. I suspected he meant me to have at least one of them, but I'd already said I wasn't drinking.

I made my way up the gangplank and along the airport's scuffed grey walkways, single, unencumbered. I looked back but he was nowhere in sight. At the first refuse bin I passed I paused. It was one of those cylindrical bins with a big rectangular mouth. I pulled Olaf's bracelet out of my pocket, hula-hooped it around my closed finger and thumb. But I kept hold of it.

The next day I wrote to Olaf's email address to order a box of ten bracelets. There was a tear-off section at the end of the leaflet for the purpose. In the white box for *Further Comment* I said the bracelets were meant for my friends, one each. I asked him, though, to consider varying the colour. Neon orange didn't go with everything. Blue or green bracelets would also be good, I wrote, or any other colour really—anything to break up the orange.

Paper Planes

TODAY, A TUESDAY AFTERNOON, Johnny and his grandmother are playing with paper planes—or, rather, he is making them and letting her hold them in her lap. Some planes are stacked on the table beside her, a collapsed ziggurat of white fragments.

The grandmother was once called Jane, though no one calls her this any more. They call her Grandma or Mrs Dent. Her two children Susan and David both call her Grandma. Johnny is Susan's child.

Johnny and his grandma are in her favourite corner—she on the stained armchair, he on the footstool beside it. Both the armchair and the footstool are nested in the dormer window of her new nursing-home room. Around the walls stand more upholstered chairs along with a pouffe and a few side-tables loaded with framed photographs, small lamps, decorative tea cups, a sea-shell collection.

This is not how the things stood in her former apartment. There, she liked her things set out in tasteful clusters and groups. Nothing stiff, nothing straight, she would say, adjusting angles, rearranging cups, scooping the shells into piles.

But now this place is her home, Susan and David tell her. This room. They say it over and over again, as if she might forget. This room and the tiny en-suite bathroom leading off it, full of obstacles that bruise her whenever she uses it, its basin, shelving, towel rail, all poking out at her—this crowded space is now her new home.

Cooked meals arrive on time, three times a day, but delivered food doesn't smell like home. Till someone reminds her she leaves the meals standing under their stainless-steel covers exuding their heavy gravy odour. Even the breakfasts smell of gravy, even that lasagne lunch right there, sat on the glass-fronted bookcase by the door, its cover half off, its edges crisping.

See, an association for every single thing you have here, Susan and David chorus, pointing at furniture they have known since they were children as if they were discovering it for the first time. The bookcase with its bubbly glass that your parents bought to mark their twenty-fifth wedding anniversary. The yellowed Penguin books on the shelves, each one signed and dated for the first time you read it, see Grandma, remember Grandma, dated again for when you used it for teaching, how clever. The Turkish pouffe splitting at the seams that Dad, John, bought in a second-hand shop and, stiffly alongside, like at home, the chunky Nineties television he also bought that she refuses to have replaced. Though her beloved piano that stood beside it in her old house, her home, is somehow, mysteriously, no longer there.

Susan took the piano for herself, leaving a post-it on the lid for the removers, *Susan*.

Grandma, I told you this before, she says, watching her mother frowning at the space beside the television.

To her brother she said at the time, If I take the piano, you take the bookcase.

But the post-it saying *David* must have fallen off, for here the thing stands, as a ledge for her meals.

See, Grandma, what a lovely meal, Susan says each time she comes in, lifting the stainless-steel cover and sniffing.

The grandmother turns away to the window.

I am half sick of shadows, she means to tell Susan, but says instead, no lunch for me today. I'll have a biscuit later when Johnny comes. For now, I'm happy looking out.

It's too much for her, Susan, says David, Having a young child around all afternoon. You've built a whole routine around it and it's too stressful for her. What if?—you know. You can't expect the carers—

Tell me what choice I have? says Susan. On Tuesdays I work late. It's not like I have a wife at home like you, to be there for the kids.

Look, Grandma, look, here's another one, Johnny now says, sitting cross-legged on the footstool. Did you see how I made it?

Her eyes are stuck on the window, the thin new birch in the garden, the hedge beyond.

Look, Grandma, Johnny says again.

He pours her a glass of water from the jug on the table. The sound of the pouring brings her back.

Yes, she nods. Yes. Why don't you show me?

She looks down at his quick, folding hands.

See how you need sharp edges, Grandma, any old paper, but sharp edges, to make the pointy shape you want.

Any old paper, she says.

Yes. Any old paper, and you fold it in half first. You can use the floor as your folding surface, see, even your lap. You line up the edges and fold the paper, then fold down the corners, to make the nose. You can use your nail to make a sharp fold, a really sharp point.

A really sharp point, she says.

Yes, really sharp. Two folds first, for the nose. Then you fold again to the centre, and then fold it in half, see, and then turn down the outer edges. Look how I slope the angle to make the wings, and now here's the arrow shape of the plane. See.

He holds it up.

And you need to throw it at once to test it, he adds. You need to throw it straight away.

But he doesn't yet throw the paper plane.

Such a thing, Johnny, she says, smiling. Such magic. To make such a thing, from this, this piece of flatness.

Yes, paper, a paper plane, the boy smiles back, and aims his plane.

The plane flies in a graceful arc across the room, strikes a chair, and nosedives to the floor. The boy darts to get it. The woman's eyes shift back to the window.

The boy straightens the bent tip, then throws the plane back to where he was sitting. His grandmother starts as it passes but keeps her eyes on the tree, the hedge. He pinches the plane's nose again, then hands it up to her.

A paper plane, she says, and lays the plane lightly in her lap, beside the snowy pile of three or four other planes. Then she takes the plane at the bottom of the pile and adds it to the flourishing hydrangea of white planes on the table beside her, spreading over her pill dispenser, box of tissues, glasses, up against the framed photograph of two children, a boy and a girl, David and Susan.

She pats the latest plane in her lap, as if to still its wings. Her veined hand flattens its folds just slightly.

So, says the boy, watching her hand. That was a good plane.

So, she stares ahead, then jolts a little, reminds herself of something. Yes, it was a good plane.

I'll make you another plane, Grandma, shall I? You liked that one, didn't you?

Another plane, yes, she says. How lovely. I'd like another plane.

That one was quite a long plane, the boy says, so it had a straight path, but with a sharp curve at the end. I'll make a shorter plane now. Like the one before. Remember, it had a rounder path?

His grandmother closes her mouth tightly, gives a tiny shake of her head.

The boy tears another piece of paper from his foolscap pad. This time he sits on the floor. He folds the paper in half, lining up the corners, then folds the corners to the centre, and then over again.

This is how I make it, with wider wings, says the boy, looking up, his hands folding blind.

Yes, I see, says the grandmother. So clever. As clever as those pilots. You know, overhead. Sending those unsinkable things.

You mean a bomber plane, Grandma, but it's not a bomber plane. It's a small plane, not even a jet.

A beautiful plane, I can see, son. A plane to fly across the world in, far over the sea.

You and me, grandma, see, flying together around the world.

He holds up the fresh plane, swoops it in front of her.

I see, my treasure, you and me. Flying around the world.

Flying, Grandma, like this, across the desert, big and hot, sand dunes below, not a cloud in the sky.

Like this, she says, taking the plane from his hand. She holds it up high, then puts it in her lap. The long plane she adds to the top of the pile. Then she takes the plane at the bottom of the pile and places it on top of the flourishing heap on the table.

Not that way, Grandma. The boy gently picks up the plane and lands it properly, skimming it down on to the table beside the glass.

So, she says. There. She folds her hands loosely over the steeple of paper planes in her lap. Where are we now?

We're far away, Grandma, really far, across the desert. So why don't I make you another plane, a plane for coming back in, a plane to catch me up with, a fast one? In case I shoot off and you want to catch me and get a ride back.

You always shoot off, says the woman. I will need another plane, a fast plane. Do you have enough, you know, what you need, the pieces, to make a fast plane?

I've got plenty, Grandma, this whole notepad, he says, his head bent, his hands pressing and folding.

He hands up the new plane and she takes it. She again holds it airborne, then places it on top of the one he gave her before, neatly, the folds slotting together. She places the other planes in her lap on top of the heap on the table but the two interlocked planes stay in her lap.

Her smile breaks suddenly into a chuckle. Her shoulders shake.

Look, she says, lightly patting the two planes. I've caught you! I've got you!

Then we try Concorde this time, the boy says, knelt over a fresh sheet of paper. But we fly together. If we still had Concorde we could travel together all over the world. We could go so fast that no one could catch us.

This time he tries three first folds instead of two. He gives the plane a curved nose by moulding the front fold between his fingernails. But Concorde is a difficult plane to get right. He crunches up the piece of paper, starts on a new one.

She places the two interlocked planes in her lap on top of the planes on the table. The pile on the table is now taller than her glass of water.

Concorde! the boy suddenly cries, holding a new plane aloft, darting it towards his grandmother.

She watches closely, then suddenly, as the plane whizzes past, plucks the under-carriage from his hand.

Here we come, sun, she says, and swoops the plane past him.

He blinks, swings with its motion, and grabs it back.

Sun, here we come, he cries.

She takes one of the planes off the pile on the table, the long plane, and flies it past Concorde.

Oh, here we come back, she cries even louder.

There is a knock. A carer in a chic grey uniform looks in.

Johnny, the carer says, your mother was stuck in traffic. She just phoned. She'll pick you up at the front if you go now, at the entrance. Time to say goodbye.

I'll come again soon, Grandma, Johnny kisses his grandma's cheek.

Come again soon, says the old woman. Tomorrow.

Then she grips his arm. But write your name first, she whispers earnestly in his ear. Write your name on the plane. On Concorde. So that I never lose you.

The carer has a pen in her pocket. The boy looks at it, the grandmother puts out her hand for it.

Write your name, Johnny, his grandmother says. And then mine beside it.

You write, Grandma. There, on that plane. You write our names. You write so nicely.

By the time she finishes writing, a spider script only Johnny could read, he is gone.

A second carer comes in, busies herself with the pill dispenser, the jug of water, the untouched plate of lunch.

The old woman places the long plane back on top of her unfurling pile of planes. Some planes, including Concorde, spill on to the floor.

Nurse, she says. She places her hand over the pile, but without pressing down on it. See this book, here, she says, this precious book that my small son made. Would you take it and put it there in the glass bookcase, with the other books?

You mean Johnny, your grandson, Mrs Dent. You mean these paper planes here?

I mean my son Johnny, yes. Who made this—this book. Please put the book side-by-side with the others on that shelf. This book is all about planes, you see, planes and going round the world. I'd like to read it again one day.

The carer separates out the planes, folds each one sharply down its central fold, so that the nose shape is partly lost, though not entirely, then squeezes the folded spindles of paper together.

See, Mrs Dent, all done for you, all neatly stacked away.

I will read it all again one day, the old woman assures her.

She leans across for her water glass. Her hand hovers searchingly over the empty space on the table.

In no time, she adds. Catch him up and bring him back.

In the bookcase the paper planes make a white sheaf that sticks out from her yellowed Penguins. The carer pushes the planes deeper in, to neaten the line, yet still they stand out, a fan of white feathers, a row of aeroplane tails queued up and waiting at an airport, ready to fly.

The grandmother bends and picks up the planes that fell down earlier. She places them on the table in the place where the heap of planes had been. Then she bends down again and picks up the crumpled paper Johnny left behind, his first attempt at a Concorde.

In her lap she smooths out the paper and folds it into thirds, following the first creases that Johnny made. She sits looking at the paper a moment. Then she folds down the edges to make the wings, pinches the front between her finger and thumb, gives the plane a bent nose.

Like Concorde, she says, and holds the plane aloft. Arriving like Concorde in no time at all.

She takes aim at the thin new tree beyond the window, its leaves stirring like feathers in the evening air. She looks around to check that she's alone. Yes, the carer has gone. The door is closed. A fresh meal is waiting under its stainless-steel cover. Its meaty smell wrinkles her nose.

She throws the plane at the window. Sun! she cries. Sun, here we come! The plane hits the glass and falls. She bends down, picks up the plane, straightens it out, throws it again. She throws the other planes still lying on the table. She throws the planes one by one at the glass till the light is gone. Then she stacks them together on the table, sits back and looks out. She can no longer see the tree. In the black glass someone is sitting, an old woman. She looks familiar and so does the glass-fronted bookcase at her back but it is hard to think quite who it is. The woman in the glass looks back. She herself doesn't seem to know.

The Park-Gate Notice

THE CONCRETE BENCH is on Lila's running route through the park. Beyond the brick gateway the route takes her along the eucalyptus-lined avenue past the grassy area where, after sun-up, a group of Indigenous people sometimes sit in a circle, through the thickets of azalea bushes along the left-hand border, and around to the dry shrubbery on the opposite side, then through the rose garden and finally over the gully. The gully is usually a dry stream bed, except for now, in the late summer, when sludgy black water clings to the reed bed. Here she takes the wooden bridge, her feet ringing on the slats, and leaves by the back brick gateway. The thrumming of her feet on the slats comes up through her legs and arms. She is aware of her bun bouncing on the top of her head, with all her fine hair pushed into it, and then of her cheeks, also slightly bouncing.

She tries to hold her cheeks still when she runs by pulling her mouth tight but today she is making an effort to run relaxed, to let her hands go floppy, feel her neck move to the pounding of her feet.

The concrete bench lies in an inset within the azalea bushes and bears a small brass plaque in memory of someone. If ever she thinks about her running route during the day, busy at the hotel reception desk, she can't recall the name on the plaque, though she sees it every time. But today there's a woman sitting on the bench, her shoulder half obscuring the plaque yet drawing attention to it, an older woman in heavy make-up, smartly dressed in pale purple.

Simon Irons, who loved this place, Lila now reads, but the woman's lavender shoulder hides Simon Irons' dates.

Lila slows and then stops, too abruptly, feels the short step jolt her left hamstring. She'll reap the effects later tonight. The woman looks up from the mouth of the white summer handbag in her lap, then clicks it closed, places it on the ground in front of her. Her red-lipstick smile makes sharp Cupid's bow points. She shuffles further down the seat, making space for Lila.

Lila shakes her head, smiling back, then stands and stretches a little, bending side to side.

'Name's Louise. Can I help you?' the woman asks.

'Sorry, no, but I was going to ask you the same question. I'm Lila.' Lila holds out her hand. 'Nichols, Lila Nichols,' she adds, just as she does every day on reception. 'Can I help *you*?'

The woman's hand clasp is hard and coldly metallic from the rings she wears on each one of her fingers. This Lila notices first, the number and coldness of her rings, and then she notices how thin the woman's arm is, and how loose the skin. Her loose-skinned arm, too, is metalled, covered in bangles and at least two watches—old-fashioned ladies' watches, thin, delicate. Her soft mottled skin hangs between the bangles like a sleeve.

She feels the woman's eyes on her face, sees the blue half-moons of her eyeshadow, the thick arcs of rouge on her cheekbones below the arches.

'You've been running,' the woman says, as if in answer to Lila's question. 'You've been running quite hard.'

'Yes,' says Lila, 'I run every evening here, in this park. I love it, the space, at this time of evening...'

She stops, not sure the woman is listening. Her wool twin-set is too warm for the weather, Lila thinks. Though, as she's running, she's not the best judge.

Was running, she reminds herself, and shouldn't stand and get cold. She stretches again, with more vigour.

But then the woman, Louise, still seated, takes her hand back, pressing her rings into her fingers.

For the first time Lila notices the large bunch of shop-bought flowers on the bench beside Louise, on the opposite side, the flowers nothing like the skinny roses in the rose garden but big, perfect cut roses, white, yellow, deep pink, scalloped like cup-cakes but with the whites slightly browning, and other flowers, too, red gerbera daisies maybe—she doesn't want to stare.

'You often run?' the woman, Louise, asks, ignoring her look.

Lila nods, she's already said so. She goes running every evening.

'Running and running,' Louise goes on. 'Running and rushing. It makes us so tired, doesn't it, this rushing and running, you hardly wonder—'

'They say it helps to keep snakes at bay, the running,' Lila says without thinking. She has never seen a snake in this park. 'Snakes are shy. The pounding of human feet frightens them away.'

Her hand is still clasped between Louise's metalled fingers and their joined arms hang looped between them.

'What would you say, my dear, my dear Lila, if I told you that I never come to the park these days, though I do know it, I know it well, and I do like it, but I never come. Just today I came.'

'I'd say that you could be missing out on a lovely place to take an evening walk,' Lila says neutrally, like talking to a guest at reception.

Louise lets Lila's hand fall.

'But you will have your reasons not to come?' Lila quickly adds.

'Of course I have my reasons,' Louise says, her voice lower than before. 'We all have our reasons. You will have your reasons, for running and running, chasing and chasing, every day, around and around this park.'

'Yes,' Lila suddenly finds she's laughing. 'Every day running and running, racing around and around. Always the same path, at the same time.'

There, she's said it again.

Louise pushes herself back on the bench, up against the concrete slats, and laughs with Lila.

'Yes, yes, the same path, the same time,' Louise laughs. 'Warding off the poor snakes. And that means you shouldn't dawdle too long now. You should be on your way.'

Lila rises up obligingly on the balls of her feet.

'I'd love to give you one of my flowers here,' Louise adds. 'As you're very nice and very young, and it's been lovely talking to you. But I think I won't. I want to keep the bunch together, intact.'

'Please keep it just as it is, it's beautiful,' Lila says, bouncing higher now. 'Nice meeting you, Louise. Maybe I'll see you here again one day.'

'Maybe,' Louise says, and waves, a quick, queenly dabble of her fingers in the air. 'Life is full of unexpected things.'

Lila continues on her usual half-circle around the rose garden but before the bridge she suddenly swerves and finds her legs retracing her path. She runs back round to the front gate, then down the avenue. An Indigenous man in jeans is dancing under one of the trees. The boom-box on the grass beside him plays rock music—Oasis, maybe. From this distance, only the bass comes through. Lila approaches the azalea shrubbery at walking pace and stops at a distance from the bench, before the last turn in the path.

Through the glossy azalea leaves she sees Louise still there, bent forwards doing something with her bouquet. The flowers are placed in front of her on the path. Whatever the thing is that she is doing, her handbag impedes her. It hangs on her thin forearm beside her bangles and sways awkwardly. Finally she puts it down and sits back. She smiles down at her feet, the handiwork she has made.

Lila steps away out of sight. Somehow the scene reassures her. Louise will be OK, she thinks. It looks like she knows what she's doing. Lila retraces her path in the opposite direction.

~

The next day the bench is empty, as always.

'Same time, same place,' Lila says to herself as she runs past, 'running and rushing.' She reminds herself not to pinch her lips or hold her cheeks so stiff.

She thinks of Louise's colourful splash here on the bench, her full bouquet of roses and gerbera daisies, her lavender twin-set and blue-and-red make-up that didn't chime. Unusual as she looked, though, she, Lila, had stopped for her. More than that, she had prompted her to laugh at herself, and that didn't often happen, or anyway not since she moved out of home and started living on her own. It surprised her, the quietness of living on her own. She'd not expected it. That she could spend all evening in her nice flat on the top floor without saying a word, her lips quietly pressed together.

To make up for yesterday's broken run Lila takes a longer path through the park, looping the grassy area and the rose garden several times before making her way to the exit. It's later than normal now and the place is almost deserted. A couple walks hand in hand on the avenue. In the evening light the roses in the rose garden look glossier than usual.

Lila runs at speed, so she doesn't at first spot the other roses, the long-stemmed, shop-bought roses lying scattered just beyond the rose garden—a few on the path, but most of them criss-crossed and awry in the gully amongst the black stubby reeds.

Who'd go tearing off the park's roses? she begins to ask herself, skipping so as not to crush the petals, and then suddenly thinks, Louise, Louise's roses. Did Louise drop the roses she was looking after?

Without breaking her stride, Lila makes to stretch down and pick up one of the roses but in the same instant sees that its petals are brown. She lets it lie. The scattering will have happened hours back, she thinks. *Scattering*—why did she think scattering? Scattering means dropping the roses here on purpose.

At the back gate her eye falls on the freshly laminated paper tied to the park fence, a new *Missing* notice alongside the other items that people hang here, the posters about the summertime kids' tug-of-war, the carols in the park beside the bowling green, the faded colour photographs of lost pets looking expectant, ready to be found. The lost ginger cat answering to the name of George Grey, or was it Ginge Gray? Last seen—. That notice the other week about a missing goldfish, Tommy, with a picture. *Lost here. Please return.* A pet with no expression at all, lost beside a dry gully bed.

The purple border around this new notice makes it stand out from the others. Positioned top and bottom is a mugshot of a woman. Not Louise, Lila checks at once, peering across the flower bed in the half-light. Can't be Louise. And then she sees, not sure if it's important, the photos are different: one is of an older and one of a younger woman, a slip of a girl, her hair blowing about her face.

As she straightens up, she sees the same notice again, immediately behind, stuck on the gate-post, and then they seem to pop out at her all over, the same purple-lined notices shining in the luminous late light, frantically distributed, fastened to the open gate itself, two of them, with grip-ties, and to the fence on the other side, stuck to the green wheelie rubbish bins at the exit, before the road, one on each bin.

MISSING.
Woman (82).
Last seen near the park wearing grey trousers.
Lucille is on Alzheimer's medication and may be confused.
She answers to several names. Lucille. Lulu. Lucy.

Along the bottom are some telephone numbers. Take a poster home, Lila thinks. She begins with the one on the fence, but the grip-ties hold firm. She has no better luck with the others she tries. The lamination is thick. The posters on the bins are stuck on with glue.

Crouching at the bins she memorises the top telephone number. She should take her mobile on runs, she thinks, in case of this kind of thing. Then she gives up. There's really no point. She checks the photos again. She doesn't recognise this woman and she can't help. It can't be Louise. That's not the shape of Louise's face, not in the top picture nor in the bottom.

Phoning would set a false trail. Louise wasn't confused.

She turns from the posters and darts back into the park. She will pick up some of the dropped roses after all, the better ones, and take them home for the nice rose-bowl vase her family gave her, a housewarming present. She can cut off the stems and have them float, like housekeeping does with the flower arrangements in the hotel lobby.

She chooses two, then three roses, drops the ones with thorns. Holding the flowers upright by the stem, she takes the path back to the exit.

The park attendant in green overalls is standing at the gate, ready to lock up. She's seen him around before though never at the gate. She holds out her flowers for inspection—see, they're not rose-garden flowers, she hasn't been damaging anything— but he is looking at the posters.

'You seen anything?' he asks, pushing at the left leaf of the gate.

She shakes her head.

'Poor lady,' says the attendant.

'Yes, poor lady,' Lila makes to go past him.

'Normally I'd be cross about all these notices but this looks like a special case. If she hasn't been found she'll be very mixed up by now, this lady. Her people will be very worried. I've looked everywhere though, under all the bushes, even in the long grass. I took my hoe and poked around.'

'Did you phone the number?' Lila asks, now outside the park, bouncing on the balls of her feet. Suddenly she wants to make sure. 'Did you tell them you looked everywhere?'

'No, not yet,' the attendant swings closed the second leaf of the gate. 'Like I said, there's nothing to report. Sure, she could still be in the park, hiding in some corner, but I don't think so. I'll check again tomorrow, I'll keep on checking. I can only imagine what it must be like for the family, for whoever put up these notices. Anyhow, you enjoy your roses.'

'I found them on the path. It's OK to take them?'

'Flowers get left. People come here to have wedding pictures done, they like the rose garden especially. They scatter rose petals, they scatter roses. I tell them off only for paper confetti. Confetti gets on to everything and stains the ground. Sometimes they leave flowers behind, teddies, other tributes. Sometimes they bring ash, you know, of dead people. The Indigenous mob don't like that so I ask people not to. But mostly I turn a blind eye. So, yes, fine, I'd have swept those roses up tomorrow.'

'If you talk to them, to Lucille's family, Lulu's family,' Lila says, still bouncing, 'If you do phone, tell them she can't have gone far. She'll be around here somewhere, I'm sure, enjoying her visit to the park, her first visit in ages. It's warm in the evenings now. It's a lovely place to take an evening walk.'

'Tomorrow, yes,' says the park attendant. 'Sure. It's kind of you to take an interest. I'll tell them that.'

Lila begins to run.

Then she hears the park attendant begin to shout. 'Hey,' he calls, 'Hey, stop. Why—How did you—?'

The sound of her feet on the gravel drowns out the rest.

Nothing she can say, she thinks to herself, no point stopping. She generally doesn't stop to talk to people on her run. Yesterday was an exception. Today was also an exception. Her job on reception means she meets strangers all day long. Her quiet time running in the park is something she needs like air. She needs it to relax her neck and empty her thoughts.

Her family thinks her job is a cinch, but in fact it takes a lot to get it right. It takes it out of her, keeping her voice steady, her face expectant, her make-up smooth, her hands neatly folded on the counter even when there's nothing much going on, when she'd rather be catching up with phone messages than watching the overhead light refracting through the glass vase that holds the floating roses paint spirals and dots and ovals and star shapes on to her skin.

Lila looks down at the roses in her hand. All the way along from the park gate the roses have been shedding their petals. What was she thinking? There's no way they'll float in water. Whoever dropped them knew they were nearly dead.

She turns in her tracks, feels that twinge again in her hamstring. She runs back. At a distance from the park gate she pauses, checks for the park attendant's green uniform. He is nowhere to be seen. The Indigenous man with the boom-box is sitting on the grassy verge in front of the gate, his back to the park. The boom-box is in his lap, silent. His eyes are closed. She approaches at walking pace. The white notices hang thickly all over the gate, flapping like prayer flags in the light breeze.

She throws the flowers over the gate and they scatter on the path. In the half-light she looks at the two photographs of the missing woman: the younger one with the hair blown about her face, the older one. For the first time she notices that the older woman is seated on a park bench that bears a small brass plaque in memory of someone. Behind the bench is a bed of azaleas in bloom. Lila looks closer but there is nothing more to be seen. The older woman could be anyone. She is almost sure she is not Louise, almost one-hundred-per-cent sure.

The Mood that I'm In

THEIR EYES MET—Paul's, Anne's—across a crowded room at the Crosskeys Retirement Home Christmas party. There were fairy lights in the plane trees over the colonnaded entrance. Their eyes locked and stayed locked. The song playing was 'The mood that I'm in', Billie Holiday singing it—the one and only version. He had it on a cassette tape that he'd made himself and played every summer driving to the beach, the children squawking in the back.

And she remembered it from—Oh, she couldn't remember, but it was her favourite song too, as they found out chatting over a scrambled-egg breakfast the following day.

Yes, it's my favourite, exactly the same, she assured him, and that's my favourite version, the one and only Billie Holiday singing it.

It was his first night out after his wife Enid's death back in the dark of the winter. They had been married fifty years and he still missed her. The kids had coaxed him to go out. Try it for an hour, Dad, have a beer and a natter. It's Christmas, after all.

As for Anne, she was there with her stepdaughter Pam, her late second husband's only child. She had been in the middle of a box-set, a thriller, good and gloomy, and hadn't wanted to come out. But then something had pushed her to the cupboard and nudged her to take out this red dress with the lace trimmings that still fitted her like a glove. In the mirror she saw she looked good in it, that the colour suited her new red hair. Also, it was festive.

Dan, her first husband, always said, you kept your teenage hipbones, Anne my love, you sexy thing. Pure sweet sixteen, even from the front.

Never dared to have your arms around me, Billie sang, and Anne got up, stretching up smoothly from the knee. She put her head to one side, and her hip pushed out the other way, turning her body into an S. Paul began to make his way towards her, striding. Making a beeline, Enid used to say. He never dropped his gaze. Left, right, he had to push aside the swinging silver Christmas lanterns tacked to the ceiling to keep his head steady, his eyes on hers.

Her first words were, 'I've been waiting for you all my life.'

He could only repeat, 'Me too, all my life.'

'I have seen your eyes before, somewhere,' she said.

He nearly said, 'Your eyes only', or some such line from some other song, but the words that came were, 'Shall we dance?'

She moved into his arms as though she had practised it. The music shifted to 'I just called to say I love you', Lionel Ritchie. Her cheek was against his, and his hand was clammy on the small of her back, her best place. Already she could feel him pressing against her. Not bad for a man of his age, she let herself think.

In the shower the next day, his shower cubicle, she was still humming the song.

Months later—long after he had soldered together the single beds in the bedroom he'd shared with Enid so they could lie entwined; long after he had given her Enid's pearl earrings, despite his daughter's clamour, because they looked so lovely against her tiny shell-like ears; long after they had spoken vows of dedication to each other in the Crosskeys Retirement Home garden, under the plane trees in full green leaf, the Korean but Baptist vicar presiding, she in the pearl earrings, his four children wearing fixed smiles; even after she had locked the door of his flat against the bothersome nurses and so-called health professionals who wanted to interfere with her loving care of him when he fell ill and began stuttering over his words; after the candle-lit dinners *à deux* in her flatlet, with dancing, and the nights watching box-sets and drinking box-wine at his place (he who had never touched wine before and had no patience with television)—they still liked to go over that first greeting at the Christmas party.

They liked to kiss and relive the electricity, Billie crooning, *Let the rhapsody of life begin,* and he would say, 'You know, my lovely loving Anne, my best love, I meant to say that night when I asked you to dance, Your eyes only, Drink to me only, all my life. I want your arms around me, all my life.'

And she would say, mouth to his ear, 'I knew you did. The words were on my lips also. Your eyes only. All my life, all our lives.'

~

In the crematorium garden after Paul's funeral Anne stands by herself at the end of the covered walkway beside the grassy remembrance garden, manoeuvring so that she is screened by the brick pillars. She watches the rest of the small party file out of the chapel. She's glad she managed to sit at the back and get away quickly. People shouldn't feel they have to talk to her. She wanted at least to spare them that.

The day is close and her green dress unfortunately shows the perspiration. It's her first time wearing it, which is more than can be said for the grim weeds of her fellow mourners there by the chapel door. From the straining jacket backs, not to mention the scuffed white patches on their knees and elbows, she can tell that these black clothes don't come out too often. And certainly no one bucks the trend by wearing green.

Thank goodness, though, she is calm and she will, if all goes well, stay this way. She will head straight home after this, to a hot bath and few more valerian pills chased down with a large g-and-t. She used the same combination after the other two funerals.

Beyond that, she will treat herself to a browse through the photos of her time with Paul—the album she put together after their last holiday, that long weekend in Blue Mountain with the big pines dropping cones on to their bungalow roof.

No one has yet made an attempt to come over, but that's fine. Most of the people are friends of Paul and Enid's from the years of their long marriage. She understands that they want to share their memories, talk about the dead. She *respects* that, as the young people say, jutting out their chins. *Respect.*

Even a bridesmaid of Enid's is here somewhere, the children said, the pretty one from the photos. Anne looked around the chapel but found no one to match the description. No doubt the woman is now as wrinkled and unrecognisable as the rest. In his last months, Paul barely saw any of these friends—perhaps occasionally Wilf and Stan on the bowling-green. And then he'd come home and complain how slow and creaky they were now.

That was how it was between them, herself and Paul, her great love, her greatest love. They were always busy together, busy and vital, busy in their togetherness, vital in their rhapsody.

A whole lifetime of loving, dancing and talking to catch up on, he used to say, and squirt more box-wine into Enid's crystal wine glasses, untouched throughout their years of marriage, and put on Anne's Billie Holiday CD, the one he ordered for her specially, the first thing he'd ever ordered online. Then he'd pull her into his arms and touch the small of her back, her best place, as he knew from that first night together.

Remembering, she smiles to herself and passes a hand across her perspiring lower back. An odd new dizziness places wispy fingers on her forehead.

She makes her way to the concrete bench closest by, avoiding the thicker clumps of grass, where her suede heels would sink away and get stained. She sees Paul's daughter approaching— Beryl, is it? Beri, the only girl, divorced, a big-hipped woman, taciturn but frank. The former husband was equally taciturn, Paul said. Of the four children, Anne knows where she stands with Beri.

'I can see you do love him,' she said, very upfront, the day they exchanged vows under the plane trees. But when Anne shut the door on the busy-body doctors Beri clammed up. These days she is, if anything, colder than her brothers.

'Sorry, Anne,' is all she now says, 'I know you will miss him terribly.'

Anne nods, tries to smile again, doesn't quite manage it. It might be the dizziness.

'Thank you for coming over, Beri,' she says. 'I am also very sorry for your loss.'

'Shall we sit down a minute?'

Anne pretends not to see Beri's hand briefly poised in the air to take her arm.

When the younger woman next speaks she is, as always, direct.

'It must feel weird, Anne, with the family here, the whole palaver. And then having done all this before.'

'Your dad was the love of my life.'

'But the whole dying thing, and then the funeral, again and again? Your first husband and then your second. And now Dad. A whole row of losses.'

'We shouldn't go into it, love, not now. Not the time. Everything ends in death, everything, so what can I say? I loved him. I will always love him. Whatever happens.'

Anne thinks of the pills in her handbag. She will take two in the taxi home and not wait for her g-and-t, she decides. She has a small bottle of water here in a side pouch. It calms her, thinking of the pills, swallowing them down with a cool drink of water.

She thinks also of the crisp white envelope slid in beside the pills. In the envelope are Enid's pearl earrings. She had thought she might give them back to Paul's kids here at the funeral, put them into Beri's large, capable hands. But now perhaps she won't. She hasn't yet written a name on the envelope. Keeping the earrings tucked away, it makes her feel somehow vigilant, watching out on Paul's behalf.

She and Beryl stare across at the funeral crowd. People are starting to say goodbye, touching shoulders and wandering over together to the parked cars. Beryl stonily bestirs herself.

'I should go. I should be over at the hall serving tea. Family is invited, Anne. You should come along.'

Anne lays a hand on her arm. Beri's forearm is a long curve, just the same as Paul's.

'I want to be clear with you, dear. I can see it's hard. I did love the others, in fact very much. The thing was—well, he would never have said it himself. No disrespect to your mother, but Paul and I, it was magic for us, you know, being together, age or no age. It was like heaven. When we were together there was no death. We didn't even think about it, death and the rest, age, illness—'

The younger woman gets up. Anne's hand drops away from her arm.

'I know all that, Anne. I know about the soldered beds. He told me about them when my pre-teen Genna was present. Your down-there blah blah blah, God knows what he was about to say. The whole business was... Well, all I can say is I'm glad it's over. Now, would you like me to arrange a lift for you, or would you like to come over to the hall for some tea?

~

It is a sunny morning, a couple of months since the funeral. Beryl stands waiting in the Crosskeys Retirement Home reception. She has come to pick up her father's final effects. Just a shoebox full, the manager said on the phone.

She presses the metal bell on the desk but it makes a thudding noise that doesn't carry and no one appears.

Her father's small flat has been sold. Her brothers hired a removal company to take away the last pieces of furniture: the pine dresser no one had space for, those soldered-together beds. After the big items were taken, a few odds and ends surfaced. The printed list is in her bag. There's a pen engraved with his name, a box of bolts and screws, a newsagent's calendar that he used to write down appointments, that kind of thing.

Believe it or not, her brothers said, after the night he met Anne, there wasn't a single appointment in the calendar. The year went blank.

Two people have joined her at the reception desk, a stooped man and a woman standing side by side. Together the three of them make a rough queue. The man punches his middle finger into the pile of *What's On* leaflets on the counter.

'I'm just so terribly worried about what's coming,' Beryl hears him say.

She steps out of the queue and sets out for the garden.

To the side of the building the phlox beds are interlaced with grassy areas in a symmetrical pattern. The gravel is freshly laid, crunchy underfoot. At each turn in the path is a bench. On the bench closest by sits a thin elderly woman with aquamarine hair. A woman with bright purple hair sits on a bench in the far corner. The Crosskeys Retirement Home colourist has been at work.

Beryl says good morning to the first woman. She ignores her. The woman pecks at a family-size bag of crisps open on the bench. She breaks the crisps into pieces on the open foil.

'Always the shortest person in the room,' the woman says to herself as Beryl crunches past, raising a triangular piece of crisp to her lips. 'That's what I've had to deal with, always, every day the same.'

Beryl sits on one of the unoccupied benches and takes out her phone. See if she still has that number of Anne's.

A male voice answers.

'Sorry, who's this?' She tries to imagine a few possible candidates to fit this voice, a neighbour, a friend. But at the same time she feels stupid, clumsy, as if she's been spotted falling on her face.

'Graham. I'm Graham, a friend of Anne's.'

'Is Anne there?'

'No, love, she had to pop out. She went to the doctor's and left her phone behind. Shall I say you called?

'Yes, please. Say it's Beryl—Beri, Paul's daughter.'

'Paul's daughter, *of course*. I've heard so much about you,

you and your brothers. You will call back, won't you? She'll appreciate hearing from you.'

'I will call back, yes. It's been a while.'

'She talks about you often, Kerry, very often, you'll be happy to hear. Paul and his children. You're all here in a photo album she often shows our friends. She scolds me mightily if I guess the names wrong.'

'Meeting people definitely helps to put names to faces,' Beryl says.

She ends the call and stares at the phone in her hands.

Our friends? Already? But she doesn't want to think this. Something hard and dry swells in her throat.

It doesn't have to change a thing, she tells herself. This Graham, whoever he is. She believes Anne when she talks about her father. A rhapsody, said Billie Holiday. She and her father had a rhapsody together. She, Beri, refuses to doubt it for a minute.

She looks up from her phone and meets the eyes of the woman with the aquamarine hair still eating crisps. A crisp square lies like a communion wafer on the woman's lower lip. Beryl motions at her own mouth, to let the woman know, but she stares on unmoved, her lower jaw working, and the fragment drops into her lap.

~

When Beryl calls back Anne is watching television.

'Switch on the news, Beri,' Anne says, 'You won't believe your eyes. A tide of plastic trash is washing up all over, right across the Indian Ocean. In Bali, Thailand, you name it, all those beautiful beaches.'

'I'm not close to the remote right now, Anne.'

'Well, it's astonishing, you must take a look later, the sand is covered with it—rubbish in heaps, water bottles, plastic twine, yoghurt pots, flip-flops, you name it, in piles and piles. They say there's a chance it could come down here too. The stuff swills around the ocean like in some toilet bowl. Fish eat it. It's terrible.'

She stops abruptly. There is a noise of wind and a commentator shouting.

'I went over to Crosskeys to pick up some odds and ends of Dad's today, Anne,' Beryl raises her voice to make herself heard over the television. 'It's nothing much but there's a pen engraved with his name. I thought you might like to have it.'

'That's so kind of you, so thoughtful,' Anne says. 'And gosh, speaking of your dad, Beri, well, this rubbish tide, they were saying earlier, it interferes with the pearl divers, you know, the young boys plunging down vast distances into the ocean, at great risk, to gather...'

Then her voice drops away and there is a scuffling sound, a long pause. When she next speaks her voice is suddenly sharper, clarified. 'I really do appreciate it. I had glue with you, Beri dear, we had glue, we got on together. In fact it should be me giving you a present.'

'That's hardly necessary, Anne. It's just an old pen of Dad's I'm talking about, with his name on it, in case you'd like to have it.'

'I'm serious, Beri. It should be me. I'd love to give you something. See, with Graham now, being with Graham, I've changed my style. You know how I liked to dress smart because your father liked a smart look. But with Graham I've got more relaxed, I've switched to brighter colours. I like to be in sync with Graham, the same as I liked to be in sync with your dad.'

'So then...?' Beryl manages to ask, very softly, but she can't think how to finish her question.

Anne doesn't notice the interruption. Beri might like to have some of her smart bits and pieces, she is saying—a nice velour scarf, a few strings of beads, just mementos really, pretty, nothing very rare or precious. She doesn't have many precious things. Come round any time to have a look.

'I never had anything valuable, Beri,' she adds, 'till your dad began to spoil me.'

Beryl hears the swish and crunch of waves on a beach, or, no, on a bank of crunchy plastic. Pearl divers, did Anne really mention *pearl* divers? Beryl imagines the slim legs of the pearl divers knotted up with plastic twine.

'Keeping in style we stay young, Beri,' Anne is saying. 'I believe that.'

'So I'll keep Dad's pen, Anne, I'm gathering?'

'Yes, that's probably right,' Anne says, and drops her voice. 'Don't take it personally, dear. You see, my memories of your father, they're locked in my heart.'

Then she speaks more loudly. 'And now you'll have to excuse me, Beri. Graham likes to watch the news without me chattering in the background the whole darned time. Isn't that what you say, Graham my dear, the whole darned time? Dear Anne, you say, God knows how you keep at it.'

~

Beryl walks out into her garden. The dew is already on the grass, shiny and cool. She walks down the path her father laid not long after she divorced James. On either side running down to the shed are the marigold borders her mother planted—to have something to do, she said, while her father was putting down the flags.

Startling, that orange of the marigolds, Beryl thinks. Startling, even spooky. Every time she looks out of the kitchen window the colour is always the same, neither more nor less, the marigolds standing orange and bright and strangely wide awake whatever the light.

She remembers her mother's broad hands tamping down the earth around the seedlings. Perhaps that's the strangest thing, the hands being gone and the marigolds still thriving like this, still glowing like lamps.

She walks down the path to the shed and the air feels heavy around her, clogged, full of solid things blocking her way. She puts her hands up to the shed wall. Its roughness gives a kind of traction.

Mother, she thinks. Mother. Father. What wouldn't she give to have them back, both of them, her mother and her father, right now, to have them close again, together again? To have back even if just for a minute or two her mother's smell and her dad's stride, and her voice and his laugh, and his long arms and her broad hands pressing the seedlings into the earth. She wants back her parents' two beds separate and side by side, though she knows how ridiculous this is, longing for everything back just the same as before. She will probably laugh at herself tomorrow, how childish she was crying for this silly moon of the past, but still she wants their lives back all together as they were before, when things felt somehow gentler than they do now.

Anne took it all away more effectively than death itself and right now Beryl hates her for it. *Hates*—it's strong. Strong, but good.

If Anne were here in the garden she, Beri, would like to grab her tiny bird-like shoulders and shake her, hatefully. She would like to throw her bead necklaces into her face and drag the pearl earrings off her small pink ears.

Oh yes, she would like to shake her so hard she wouldn't forget it, even though she is sure Anne hardly cares one way or another what she thinks, that from the day of the funeral she has barely spared her a thought.

Thinking this, Beryl hates her more. She hates her for these terrible feelings sweeping through her, these patches of heat prickling in the crook of her elbows, in her palms. She hates Anne for making her feel helpless, hapless, clumsy, from the very night of the Crosskeys Christmas party. She hates her for wrong-footing her.

So, Anne, she'd like to tell her after shaking her, here's what I wanted to say from that very first day. Your dance with him, I hate you for that, for that especially. For how special it was to him, for how graceful you were. From the hundred times he told me about it, every move is inked into my memory. I can see how you took that dance all for yourself. I see the thrust of your red hip, and the curve of your body. I see how he came walking over to you and I'm in your place. I see his head weaving its way through the hanging Christmas lanterns and, though it's stupid, I want a dance like the one you are about to begin—a dance with a dancer like my dad. I mean, not my dad, but *like* my dad. I want someone to catch me around my waist, and sweep me lightly onto the dance floor like Dad did you.

I see every move that you made in his arms and I envy you.

Beryl hears the phone ring and then stop. She straightens anyway and takes her hands away from the shed wall. Genna, she thinks, her phone out of credit, calling for a lift home. She should go in.

Mysteriously, she feels a little better, better for the creosote smell on her palms and the orange marigold lamps still glowing at her feet and this good strong hatred pulsing through her heart.

The windows of the house reflect the colours of the evening sky. Something flashes across the glass, a blink of the light, a passing bird, probably. She knows there is no one indoors.

She scrubs at her wet cheeks with the backs of her hands, the skin that is free of creosote smell, and walks up the path.

She finds she is humming something, must be a dance song, dah-da-da, she can't quite place it or locate the words. She takes a few small steps anyway, right, left, left, dah-da-da, and spins herself around. The bright windows wind marigold scarves around her head.

~

In the church yard after Graham's funeral Anne stands to the side of the main group of mourners. A dusty yew tree pokes its dry twigs into her shoulder. This time there are no relatives or children to avoid—Graham was her first partner without children—but she doesn't in any case want to draw attention. At home she took her usual cocktail of valerian pills with gin, a double shot, to still her dizziness. No day is free of dizziness now. And she has worn black, just the same as all the others, an old dress that has seen several funerals, the same as all these other weeds.

She puts a finger to her ears, checking the warm feel of her pearl earrings—Paul's pearl earrings. The earrings are the only thing she has on that's not black. They are still the most delicate and the most precious thing she owns. Graham was well off and generous, but not open-hearted in the way Paul was—not in life anyway. In death, well, in death it has been different, very. She's still—

You only live once, Graham would say, scrolling the hiking-holiday sites on TripAdvisor. You're a past master, Annie, come help me spend my money.

She thought he meant *then*, naturally, spending his money in that moment then that he always talked about seizing. She didn't think, never could have thought, he meant spending long-term, spending his money then, and also now, beyond the grave.

Her black outfit hasn't warded off rude stares from people

here on the cemetery path, now that they're out in the daylight. Well, whoever they are, Graham had no use for his old acquaintances, he said so himself, and, if they stare like this, she has no use for them either. So-called old friends from my work days, he used to say, and I mean *old* friends, Annie, they don't keep up with me like you do, do they, more ways than one?

After they met, she and Graham—they were both waiting in the queue at the optician's, two young-old people fated to cross paths, he later said, two young spirits wanting to drink life to its very dregs—after that, he no longer much contacted his old friends. They, she and Graham, spent every day they could keeping busy, hiking the trails and visiting the sites he had wanted to see all his working life, but had never had the time. They hiked River Hill, Rocky Point, Wild Valley, Grace Cliffs, all the best rambling and coasteering resorts—the more remote the route the better, and the more luxurious the hotel. She learned to enjoy hiking. She was nimble, after all. Afterwards, she always had a facial booked. As for coasteering, she waved him off, then retreated to the spa.

It was coasteering that had taken him, an unexpected slip and fall one day at Grace Cliffs, a fall that brought on a sudden heart attack, and then, by the time they got to hospital, another, the fatal one, an unimaginable two weeks ago.

Still, nothing can take away the memories of the fun they'd had together, the enormous fun, she'll never forget it, she'll always be grateful. As for the other business, grateful doesn't quite do it. Greatful would be better. *Great*ful. No word quite big enough.

No word for it, eh Beryl, Anne says to herself. She remembers how nice it was at Paul's funeral when Beri came rolling big-hipped out of the group of mourners. She'd like it if she were here now, a friendly face to talk to, share her news. She'd assure her, of course, your father, he was my best love, but

Graham, oh gosh, he was so here, there and everywhere, and he made me laugh. Together we laughed at life.

Cheers, my darling, he'd say, clinking my glass, why wouldn't beautiful old girls like you fall for wrinkled old fellows like me? We're gold, aren't we, we're solid gold.

I remonstrated with him, Beri, of course I did. I enjoyed his company like I enjoyed Paul's, my dancer. But he shut me up, he put his finger on my lips.

Not a word, Annie, he said, I'd do it, too, if I were you. Who wouldn't go for gold, eh, old gold, someone with your talents? In my shoes, who wouldn't give their life and heart and everything they own for holding you, you leathery, impossibly sexy thing.

I cried like a baby, Beri, when I opened the lawyer's letter. He'd left it all to me, everything, every bit. More than unimaginable. Never before.

Anne is crying now. She stands closer to the yew tree. It's the thought of him lying crumpled like a bit of rubbish at the base of that slippery rock, so helpless and ruined, that breaks her up. And the thought that it must have been just days—a mere few days—after he changed his will.

She touches the wetness on her cheeks with her wrists, so as not to mess her make-up. If Beri were here, she might give her a tissue. She has not brought tissues herself. No need. She has never before cried at a funeral.

People begin to wander off in the direction of the parking lot. Anne sees the broad back of the former colleague who gave the eulogy, so-called—just five minutes it was, just a few words really. Could have been anyone. What a hard worker Graham had been. What a mate. *Had been*, is no more. The mate hadn't shed a tear.

Where the main group was standing, a mound of earth covered in squares of AstroTurf like carpet samples is almost visible. Anne turns away. Something odd and bright crosses her vision, and she is suddenly dizzy again, dizzy enough to grab on to a bit of yew to stop toppling over.

Had been, it's hard to hold in her head.

She makes her way to a fold-out canvas chair some mourner has left behind. It's the only place to sit. If Beri had been here, *had been*—if Beri *were* here, she, Anne, would ask her to come over and have a ·chat, sit down on the grass here beside the chair, the real grass, that is, not the stuff on the mound, and then she'd try telling her what happens next.

Beri would listen of course. She'd say that for Paul's girl, she is the listening type, the kind, wide-hipped sort of woman who, however, never keeps her man.

Come, Anne, she imagines Beri saying, maybe patting her knee, tell me what you dream of doing? Now, you know, you have all that money.

And Anne tells her. She sits up, takes a gulp of air—an old lady gesture, she knows, a gobble, she really shouldn't do it—and she tries to tell Beri everything. It's tough though. As soon as she gets going, she stumbles. There's so much to say and she wants to say it all at once. It's hard to keep the words in order. Silly stuff comes out of her mouth, debris, as if she's sleep-talking, none of it making sense, she can tell. She tries to go slower. There are a few people lingering around the mound. Were they the ones staring earlier? She'd hate to draw their attention now.

There, Anne, Beri says soothingly. Don't mind them. Now she really does pat her knee. Take a moment, steady on.

A cruise, Anne says, I dream of taking a cruise—east, north, all over. Across the ocean you can get to anywhere. Graham's holidays, they were landlocked, and see, he was killed by a rock. I want to visit places across the ocean, I don't even know their names. Those beautiful beaches on television, while they are still clean, I want to visit the beaches that are still clean. Those islands like treasure islands that poke straight up out of the water. I want to dance on deck the way I danced with your father. The stars like a canopy overhead, the equator underfoot. I want to dance while crossing the equator.

For some reason people really are looking at her now, the people still beside the mound. They are looking round, they are walking towards her, their faces frowning. She must speed up.

Top of the list, Beri, she says more softly, her finger at her lips, are those diving boys, the pearl divers. I want to take my cruise to the places where the pearl divers work, where the pearls come from. Those boys train themselves to dive straight and deep, full fathom five, they learn to hold their breath till their lungs nearly burst. Sometimes they do burst, there is a mishap, they don't make it. They drown. Imagine, Beri, your pearl earrings, our pearl earrings, came from a boy who drowned while diving, who whooshed up to the surface with the closed oysters still clutched in his dead hands.

There is a rush to Anne's chair. The first person to reach her catches her drooping arm, and with his other hand clasps her around her waist.

'My best love,' Anne says, straight into his eyes, 'my dancer.'

Her head moves to his shoulder and his gentle hand goes to the small of her back and holds her there.

The Biographer and the Wife

I
The biographer

The writer is late. He takes long strides across the wet forecourt to the entrance doors suddenly plush with red carpet, shining glass, theatre lights. Crap, he is later than he thought. The noise of the company has receded to a distant murmur. But for two security guards in tailored black, everyone has gone through.

He straightens his black tie, his hand goes to his nape, the bristly line of this afternoon's cut. It reassures him. Already he can imagine the widened eyes and annoyed looks around the table. He's seen it before, writers more recognised and garlanded than he tacitly assuming the right to deal out judgements, as if literary composure were chiefly to be expressed through the handing down of censure.

Except that tonight, he reminds himself, he counts for something. He is himself on a judging panel, though the prize is a minor one. His fellow panellists will be elsewhere in the room. His breast-pocket is full of newly printed business cards with crisp edges. He will make the most of the evening, his red velvet seat alongside Professor this or Doctor that, under that glittering roof he has till now only ever seen on television, that vast hall where, he notices glancing back as one of the black-clad guards slides his coat off his shoulders, the bright arc-lights are already torching the stained-glass windows violet and red.

To the blonde in black at the chrome barrier taking names, he breathes 'Traffic', and then 'Sorry', though his name doesn't at first seem to appear on her list, and must be spelled and re-spelled.

'Ah, here. Don't worry. It takes ages for people to find their seats.'

'There'll be a bottleneck, I anticipate,' he tries a smile. 'Could I slip in without a fuss, perhaps if there's a short cut?'

'Josh,' calls the woman, taking pity.

The security guard, his coat still in his arms, comes over.

The writer sets off a few steps behind the security guard down a passage at an angle to the noise and light. They reach lino-covered stairs with the look of backstage, plastic-covered banisters, scuffed walls.

'Down the stairs, one flight, can't go further, corridor to the right takes you to the side entrance,' the security guard says at a gallop, refusing to look at him for some reason, his eyes directed slantwise down the stairs.

'Thanks, mate, I appreciate it,' the writer says to the guard's retreating back.

It's a chance, is his main thought—make the most of it. Not to arrive last after all.

He takes the stairs two at a time, once or twice almost

losing his footing, sliding down an extra step. He skids on to the next landing, panting hard. The black eyeball of a security camera ogles at him. He feels suddenly, inexplicably, on edge and agitated, like a trespasser, stumbling in where he has no business.

There is one other person on the landing, or, no, two—two people, a tall man in an expensive suit, a face he knows he has seen before, and some flunky hovering in his shadow.

He nods briefly, then looks away embarrassed. He should know who this man is, that high forehead, narrow-bridged nose. He'd recognise that nose anywhere…

He turns to look where the other two are looking. The red floor numbers on the panel over the lift door mark its descent. *1, 0, -1.* He touches his bow tie and his hairline. An arriving lift means opportunity, fresh chances, perhaps some fellow guests, similarly belated.

Looking up, the identity of the guy flashes through him. He's that MP, one of those penny-pinching scrooge-type politicians who cut funds to everything that makes life enjoyable while keeping his own pockets lined. And here he stands—the writer restrains himself from taking another look—a man of culture, seemingly, taller than he had imagined, thinner, too, debonair in his fine grey suit, looking as though he doled out money to the arts every day.

The lift ping-pings, a fragment of Morse code. The politician puts a smile on his face. The writer catches the movement in the corner of his eye. Involuntarily he, too, stands up straight, at attention.

The lift doors slide open. From its illuminated alcove rolls a wheelchair bearing a man with a massive head atop mighty shoulders. Behind is a burning nest of golden hair, a slender, towering woman pushing the wheelchair, and, to the side, an assistant helping to steer.

The politician steps forward with his arms outstretched, his sleeve just brushing the writer's, and, as he does so, the writer shifts his weight and so is caught up within the party of three now revealed to the trinity in the lift as to all intents and purposes part of the waiting tableau.

The air is suddenly a-hum with laughter, warmed perfume. Light glances off jewels and stainless steel. Names are called. The writer catches a name that he has only ever heard on the radio, the name of another writer, a very great writer. Ah yes, of course!—he knew that he recognised him.

Now he quickly draws back, pushes himself up against the side of the lift door. Chances like this come but once... From this side-angle he has a view straight down on to the bulky figure in the wheelchair, the politician now bent down to him, his arms around his shoulders. The writer can see the famous silver quiff —wouldn't he recognise it anywhere?—and, beneath, the uplifted face, the twisted, sensitive mouth and hooded eyes. He sees the long bejewelled hand on the great man's shoulder lightly touch the politician even as he is hugged, the hand of the tall woman in red velvet with the burning hair who is pushing the wheelchair. Yes, he has read about her, he knows her name, the young wife who, at this very instant, looks straight at him, the writer, sees him even as she is seen, and nods.

Physical love, to me it's like meat. The line from the interview the great man gave shoots into the writer's memory, the rare interview just prior to his last marriage, his third, to this burning woman, his wife.

Physical love, to me it's like meat is to another man. I cannot do without it. In her alone I have found my match. My meat and my bread.

In her alone. The writer stares into the wife's face, but her eyes have dropped away. The politician has drawn upright, somehow still holding the great man's hand, and the assistant is taking the handle of the wheelchair from the woman's long fingers, but no, she presses her to one side and swings the wheelchair in the direction of the red passageway that extends smooth and empty towards the distant hubbub. The silver quiff disappears behind her arm. Every hair on the writer's body stands on end. A ball of energy has rolled from the lift and caught him in its burning. He has no choice, he steps into her wake.

The politician to his left, the assistant and the security detail a little ahead, the writer keeps within their bubble. No one gives him another look. Her red velvet dress drags a little on the carpet. He takes care not to step on it yet to remain in step. Stay with them. He feels his neck, his jaw, might snap he feels so turned on, so up.

In fact, he now knows or recalls, there is no writer he admires more. This great man is a son of his soil. His work has given word and voice to the expanses of his sere land that no one else has found before him. From other writers, himself included, the sensations slip away like oil. The great man collects that oil and gives it shape and form in vessels of bone and rock. Years ago, didn't he write to him and say this, or words like it? Or, if he didn't, he should have. He should write them down now, tomorrow.

He imagines the young wife opening the great man's fan mail, smoothing the pages with those long, manicured hands, filing the praise away in special boxes to be kept for those moments when his spirits fall and the dark cloud descends, as the great man has himself written, the cloud that grows in darkness as his years increase.

See here, he imagines her saying to the great man, smoothing the pages, see this moving tribute, *vessels of bone and rock*, isn't it just right?

Halfway down the passage the party halts.

'My shoes,' the young wife laughs and shrugs apologetically at the politician. She lifts her hem slightly to reveal the ballet slippers she is wearing. The writer wants to step forward and shield her from his gaze.

The assistant hands her a drawstring bag, high leopard-skin heels protruding from its mouth, and points down the corridor in the direction from which they've come. The wife bends and whispers something quick and low in the great man's ear. As she comes past the writer, the flow of her movement stirs his hair.

It's his chance, before anyone else can get in. She created the possibility, she conferred it, an unconscious blessing.

With one hand he takes the wheelchair handle still warm from her touch. He swivels the wheels part-way round and drops down on one knee in front of the old man. The politician and the flunky step closer. The politician's hand is on the writer's shoulder but the old man makes a gesture and the hand falls away. The writer extends his free hand. He presses his freshly cut business card into the great man's palm.

Words gush from his mouth—strong, powerful words about his visionary work, about soil, shape, form, bone. Thank you for the work, I've loved it always, the dark and bitter passion, the wry irony. I've got up with it in the morning. I've gone to bed with it at night.

A new tableau has formed around them. The writer sees the young wife come striding back in her leopard-skin heels, standing even taller than before, her hair aglow under the lamps. He sees the scene as she sees it, the attendants respectfully inclining from right and left, the man at her husband's feet presenting his homage.

He sees, as she does, the old man's eyes melt. He has learned to crave praise, as the writer felt he would. His mouth working as he listens, the great writer reaches into the lesser writer's heart, and lays hold of his admiration, his devotion, but something more again, critical consideration honed through a lifetime of diligent study. The writer sees, as she sees, that the great man has endured the days of his old age in a wheelchair pushed by his radiant wife on account of this type of tribute, that tumbles into his lap unsolicited and yet that he commands.

But there is more. The writer sees the great writer uncover that thing within him he did not want to hide and yet wanted him, this reader of men, to find in him—not discernment alone but a matching ambition, a reciprocal intelligence, or close to it; in short, something of greatness, a mind that might complement his. He wanted him, the great writer, to discover within him, the lesser, a talent who might nonetheless draw him out, might paint his portrait in prose, so that he might contribute—with her help, he trusted, with her inspiration—his small portion to the annals of the greats, so that the generations would go on reading him, the great man, as they would thus read the lesser, and the lesser the great.

The writer, the *life writer*, as his crisp card says, feels her eyes still on him, looks up and is differently touched again.

She, the wife, is looking at him with new recognition. Her unblinking eyes are finding within him the architect of her husband's reputation, the custodian of his future. He knows she cannot be part of a future that will forget his work.

Therefore, he, the younger writer, life writer, biographer—self-appointed but soon to be authorised—will forthwith vault into the future on the shoulders of the giant, and the young wife will jump with him because she loves the man, the great writer and the man. The story of their love will be placed in the biographer's safekeeping—already she knows it, feels it. With the passionate fire that ignites the great man's late work, he, the biographer, will re-illumine the earlier. He will learn to understand this energy from the inside, this fireball of energy that has caught them both, the great man and the wife, in its burning.

The closing lines of the interview come back to him.

I looked for love in a desert world and only now have I uncovered it. I have uncovered it and will hold it and I will die in its embrace.

Writer, his card says it, *life writer.* The politician has taken the card from the great man and looks at it with approval. He nods lightly at the assistant. At that moment the great man's hand falls momentarily on the writer's, the new biographer's shoulder.

His life story of the great man, the writer knows in that instant, will open with this moment of his anointing on a red carpet, under these yellow lamps, surrounded by these key witnesses, with the great man's hand upon him.

Yes, he could not have imagined it, there was a touch, a sudden pressure on his shoulder, she saw it, too, as the great writer bestowed his consent.

'We should get a move on,' the wife says, and takes the wheelchair. 'Do join us, Mr— . Everyone will be waiting for us to get seated. They are about to say grace.'

II
The wife

It was cold that winter, the kind of dank unforgiving cold that clings to the skin and penetrates even wood, even the warm oak floorboards we had specially fitted the first summer we were married. Night after night rain lashed the windows on the west side of the house, it seemed horizontally, and the run-off from the blocked gutters—blocked since his last illness—coated the walls in trails of green slime.

It was the second winter following his death and, if

anything, I found it longer and harder than the first—the nights longer and darker, the days sludgy. I had enough to do, the legacy to arrange, the papers and photographs that had stacked up across his last years still to file, but everything took an age, as if there were leaden weights attached to my limbs, my mind.

Just a few months before, at the end of the summer, I had signed the contract to write my memoir, a narrative of our time together. I had thought it would lift my spirits. Already I saw how I'd set up the storyline, a Z-to-A reverse chronology, beginning before his final short decline and ending with the first time we met, at that out-of-the-way literary festival on the island—he the famous author scattering upon the event a little of his stardust; myself the volunteer, the gopher. Already I had written the opening yet closing scenes, our last holiday in Europe together, in Arles among the baking lavender fields. What better setting for the long honeymoon that lasted our whole marriage?

But then I got stuck. Something in me resisted going backwards. Yet telling the story the other way about, directed into the future, meant moving the narrative arc inexorably towards his death.

I could not face his death, literally and in all other ways. I could not move our story in that direction. He had stepped off our beautiful path together without giving me so much as a warning and, even two years on, I could not face going onwards alone. I could not bear the thought of talking to him out loud or in my head and never getting a response. I did not want to be a *widow*—that sad, dragging word.

Two years on, busy as I was, the dark days in our clammy house still congealed my blood and the nights killed me. It wasn't just how everything still spoke of him—the trinkets he had collected on our travels, the pots and pans he used to cook his winter stews, how these things all clanged dully gone-gone-gone, like an off-key cymbal. It was the nights. The nights were still full of him—which is to say, full of the terrible dream of him that took me every night in its arms.

Unless I took a sleeping pill, the dream each time caught me in a horrifying loop, a terrible rerun of his last night alive. It began with our usual embrace, tenderly, like all our nights together, but then moments later I was suddenly pinned down, suffocating in my own bed, our own bed. There I lay, covered in cold sweat, held down, grappling him, and he was prone on top of me, a cold dead hulk steadily stiffening, a cold dead skull with the jaw askew, my husband yet not my husband, the spirit departed, who knows how, by some sudden stroke, even as I slept.

Could you not have warned me, Klaus, awakened me, before you left me with the shell of you in my arms?

This terrible nightmare would not let me go. Whenever my guard was down the flashbacks came without warning—even now, at this moment, at our friend Jonathan's housewarming party, here in his graceful new bungalow with the picture windows down the side of the lounge facing the bay.

I stood on my own, holding the glass of sparkling wine Jonathan had just given me and admiring the view—the pale creamy sea, the thin nimbus clouds, the sky blueing towards evening. I was wearing a new white dress with tapering sleeves and a round neck, my hair in tight plaits, a Grecian look Klaus loved in me—fit for the Elgin Marbles, he always said. And then, without warning, even as I looked out, traced the soft wave pulses pushing into the bay, my body ran cold sweat and I felt the dead weight on top of me. It should have been a sign.

At that same moment I saw the biographer. I saw the biographer before I recognised him, if I can put it that way, though his agent had already once brought him to the house.

I found him looking at me across the room and nodding in greeting over the heads of the other guests, for we were both tall. I did not nod back, not yet, I was still trying to place him—that wide forehead, the wine-reddened lips—but even as I stood there, looking back, I was overcome with memories. I remembered the red-carpeted corridor on the way to the prize-giving in the great hall, the ceremony culminating in the lifetime achievement award that Klaus had sensed would be his last. I saw the welcome party waiting on the landing, the solicitous minister at its head, and then, yes, a man, this man, falling to his knee before Klaus's wheelchair.

Even as I stood caught in this rush of memories, the biographer set off across the room towards me. Like a tank he ploughed a straight path across the carpet, not once dropping his eyes. This was the moment to turn away—Jonathan was close by, still pouring wine, popping a cork—and yet, even as the writer bore down on me, something I cannot explain writhed through my innards and unsettled me.

'Eve, how wonderful to see you,' the biographer, I will call him Will, said. His hair, combed in a thick iron-grey wave, fell back from his face as he raised his chin to greet me. And yes, I remembered now, connecting that uplifted face and that low-timbred voice, how he had looked at Klaus with the same open expression, looked up at him with these same reverential words, and so wooed him.

In the same minute, even as he said my name, and I said the usual things in return, I realised, too late, that I should not have dressed in this way, with the Grecian plaits spread across my bare shoulder-blades, as if he, my husband, were still there to admire me. Yet he was not there, would never be again, he had sidestepped our path together, while the biographer, Will, who even today, yesterday, last night, had been poring over Klaus's lines, digging into them for as-yet-uncovered meaning, stood appraising me, following with his eyes the Grecian lines of my hair and gown.

'I hoped you'd be here,' he was saying when next I concentrated. He seemed to be smiling. 'I wanted to talk, catch up. As we're working on related projects, if I can put it that way.'

He knew about my book! Someone had told him, though the ink on the contract was barely dry. It felt suddenly as if we were stuck in the same small room together, the same library carrel, as if an invisible mischievous hand had shoved us in there, inescapably side by side like dolls in a doll's house.

He was too close. I made to step back, smile vacantly, deny everything, but then I saw again Klaus's hand on this man's shoulder, how he let it rest, gripped it tight. How grateful I had felt at the look of relief in Klaus's face that night.

All evening it had been tough to calm Klaus down, I remembered. He was a worrier by nature, but in the taxi on the way to the prize-giving his anxiety got the better even of me. His fidgeting kept dishevelling his black tie and our assistant kept straightening it, till finally even I, his unswerving wife, began to feel uncertain. I asked him to stop fretting.

'*Of course* I'm fretting,' he exploded, his lame leg restless. 'Isn't it a lifetime achievement award, the culmination of my life in letters? Haven't I been waiting for it forever? But I don't feel culminated. I'm not rounded out. Might they not pronounce me insufficiently achieved and at the last minute withdraw the award?'

Life was cruel, he went on, it had reduced him to this wheelchair, and the last book had been so difficult to finish, the plot lines snarling, even towards the end, the minor characters staying flat, uninteresting, even now he doubted—

And then, as I was pushing him along, because it helped him to feel my hands on the chair, this devotee had dropped down on his knee in front of him, and his brow had cleared.

As soon as we got home that night, the glass trophy in my lap, Klaus had gone to his computer and looked up the biographer—the life writer, as he called himself. Klaus straight away pronounced him of his tribe, an impassioned realist. He called his agent first thing the next morning and arranged a meeting. Will's ambitious study of the folk poet Reinhardt Kester had appeared only months before, a portrait that painted this small-town university professor with a side-line in verse as a provincial Rilke. The biography was, my husband said the reviews said, one in a thousand.

After that he invited him home, just the once, but the visit lasted for hours. Klaus brought out his favourite Pinot Noir from the cool place under the south-facing verandah. He showed Will his study—the big desk purpose-built to fit the wheelchair behind it; the numbered archive boxes he had had specially made by the restorers at the state library; my photograph hanging opposite where he could always see it; the glass trophy; the other small contrivances to help his writing, like the piles of taped euro coins, saved from our honeymoon, that elevated his keyboard.

'Don't you think, Eve?' the biographer was now saying, his voice raised. 'Let's compare notes. He's a big enough subject for more than one study, I hardly need to tell you. As we're here, shall we arrange something?'

'Now?' I found myself saying.

In reply he took his phone out of his pocket, pressed the diary app. 'It would be great to talk.'

I felt for my purse, paper, a pencil. His eyes followed my hands patting my sides. He seemed to be leaning into me, bending over me even, though I am easily as tall. Again the worm in the base of my belly stirred.

He went on talking, but hardly a word went in. There was something about the light from the sea, and coincidental and fortuitous meetings, and about starting a new chapter centred on the remarkable short novel Klaus had completed not long before he met me, *Yonville*, a sequel to *Emma Bovary*, in which Emma did not die but found a third lover, a rich man to settle all her debts.

'Don't you agree, Eve, it was so surprisingly light for Klaus, so frothy and sexy, fantastic really for a writer of his seasoned maturity, his gravitas, how did he do it?'

And he paused, his reddened lips puffy, waiting for me to say something. For the third time something in my guts turned.

The following week we went out to dinner, an Italian place with a first-floor balcony, rough-hewn tables, black cladding on the walls. Though it was a warm night for winter the open balcony doors let in a draught. I was glad of my long-sleeved jersey dress, its high turtleneck collar.

About our conversation I remember hardly a thing, just the very ordinary pasta arrabiata, and something he said about biography, the question of whether biography was the new fiction. I remember also the raw, stupid, indiscriminate desire again plucking at my guts.

Then the decaf espressos arrived and he came at last to his point. He wanted to ask me a few things, he said, not interview me *per se*, but rather confirm stories heard elsewhere. Speaking of coincidences, as we did, you know, last time—did we? I asked myself—he wondered about the things that had drawn Klaus and I together at first, you know, *after* the festival where we met, when we got talking. He had heard that we both loved birds and bird-watching, that we shared wide-ranging tastes in music, Handel, Bach, but also the Grateful Dead, Little Feat—

But how did he know these things? I asked myself. I had typed up some of these details, of course, but I was the wife, the widow. I let him bridge his own pause. I looked at his hands clasping his coffee cup, his rosy, supple hands with their big-knuckled fingers. I had to clasp my own hands together in my lap, the urge to grip those fingers was so strong.

Holding me tight in bed at night, Klaus had always said there will be others. I would not want you to be alone. Sunk in the dank cavern of my grief, I had many times remembered this. His words sanctioned me now. I did so want to be touched, to be held. I wanted the side of Will's hand there to slide up hard and warm between my thighs.

'In a way, the timing couldn't be more perfect,' he was saying. 'I don't mean we join forces necessarily, but at least set up a regular conversation, exchange tips. It makes sense, writing in tandem about the same subject, excited about the same life, but from different perspectives, obviously.'

I managed to repeat back to him, 'A regular conversation, yes. From different perspectives.'

'You'll excuse me for saying this,' he went on, 'but some of the research I do might be useful to you. Much of his life must have felt like past history from where you stood.'

His book would ingest mine, I then saw. It would suck it in. My memoir, my memories, the few notes I had got down so far, would be his *material*, his substance, his meat. He was telling the story that was mine to tell, he wanted to tell it back to me. I saw it coming and yet I did nothing. My innards craved him like food.

Two nights later we again met for dinner. It was at the same restaurant, perhaps it was the same pasta arrabiata. I wore the same turtleneck, with my hair in Grecian plaits. By midnight, we were in his flat, in his huge bed with its crisp white sheets, and I was held tight, as I had wanted. In fact I was held too tight. His powerful arms engulfed me. His hands scalded my skin.

'Hold on, Will,' I had to ask at one point, 'Take a break, let me breathe.'

But when he pushed back, withheld himself, things were

worse. Now I could not avoid his eyes, that gimlet stare fixed on me, even when he came.

Still, that was the first sedative-free night since Klaus's death that the nightmare did not visit me.

After that night we spent every Sunday together. We visited art exhibitions and craft fairs, and took drives through the small dry towns scattered along the peninsula. Afterwards we always ended up back at his place, on his crisply laundered sheets. Each time I brought along a fresh change of clothes and showered and changed before dawn, arriving back on my own doorstep, Klaus and my doorstep, as the new day broke, ready for a new week's work. And I was at last working. Writing came from my pen in fits and starts, a memory here, an image there, and the draft of my first chapter slowly grew in length.

Yet all this time Will avoided returning to the topic of our conjoined projects, the things we might exchange. He took down no notes and his bedroom was free of recording devices—I did check. Generally it was I who introduced the subject of Klaus, if I was reminded of him, and he responded in a warm, kindly way, without probing. He left his mobile phone on his hallway table every time he came in.

In fact we talked very little, even on our long afternoon drives. I spent the greater part of these excursions thinking about the sex we would later have. After that first night, our coupling was always scissored, distracted, our torsos as far apart as a ninety-degree angle makes possible. But it was good to be held, at least for that early period we spent together. True, at night, if I ever awoke, I often caught his open eyes on me, shining in the light coming in from the street. It was the price I had to pay for being held. Every time, I quickly shut my eyes again, tried to fall back to sleep. The memory of his watching only ever came to back to me much later, long after I was home.

By and by the time came for him to come to our house

and it was then that things changed. Of course I had prepared everything carefully. I aired the spare room and refreshed the sheets. I locked the cabinets and cupboards that held Klaus's papers and sent the completed box files of his early work to the national library for safekeeping. Our cute *his and hers* kitchen stuff that we had so enjoyed using, the mugs, plates and aprons, I hid in the pantry. I wedged our bedroom door shut and fitted a padlock to the inside of Klaus's study door. Then I locked up the study and let myself out through the sash window and jammed that shut too.

The first night I made a fire and we drank a bottle of Klaus's Pinot Noir. Will said we didn't have to have sex, we could just talk. I led him to the spare bed anyway, but then my body locked shut, I could not let him in. The night was wakeful for us both. Several times I glanced across and saw his eyes shining up at the ceiling. Later I must have fallen asleep because when I woke suddenly around dawn, I was alone in the clammy cold bed, and there were stirrings all through the house, creakings, rattlings, tappings.

'Talk to me,' Will said the second night, this time at table. 'Tell me how this feels to you, my being here, holding you in this space, loving you?'

I turned my face away. He should have not said *loving*. It was a mistake. After coffee I asked him to leave.

He did not return to the house and yet my work began to suffer. Some days I wrote a paragraph where before I had written pages; some days I wrote nothing at all. I could no longer find my way through to the Z-to-A story-line. Will was in the road. Whenever I wrote about Klaus, even the best times—the evenings we spent by the fire reading from his new work, the walks we took before his leg got bad—it was Will with his eyes gleaming in the darkness I saw in his stead. With every word, Klaus retreated from me.

Will and I agreed to a daytime meeting in a neutral place, the café beside the art gallery. I asked him not to touch me, yet I could not avoid his eyes.

'I'm in very deep, Eve,' he said, or words to that effect. 'Klaus once talked about love fiercer than death, about never letting it go. I don't want to say this, but I must say it, I feel this love for you. I love you and desire you more than anyone I've ever loved before.'

It was then I saw that Will didn't only want me for material. He didn't only want the woman Klaus had loved, the mere mortal coil of this woman. He wanted things that went beyond that, far beyond. He wanted to feel the desire that Klaus had quickened in me. He wanted somehow to fill the place that Klaus had occupied in me. He wanted to reach in, probe, dig around, and then take that place. Watching me at night, he was considering his chances, how to effect the grab. He had me wanting him and he wanted my spirit in exchange.

So I broke things off. On the phone I asked him to stop everything, the calls, the texts, the deliveries of flowers. He came to remonstrate on the verandah, his arm propped across the door frame. I managed to shut the door on him. Then he stood for hours in the street, rocking back and forth, shouting my name. He returned the following night, and the night after that. On the first two nights I begged him by SMS to stop. On the third night I called the police.

The following morning I called my agent. Will's biography of Klaus was no longer authorised, I said. I wished to withdraw authorisation. I was Klaus's literary executor, I could do this. My agent asked for reasons. One very good reason, I said—his methods are unsound.

It is another year on now. I am still on my own. Perhaps I will always be. At night the dream of Klaus still comes to me. I am held, yes, but by a ghost, the dream of a ghost.

At parties I occasionally meet someone—mostly men, on occasion a woman. When we spend the night together it is usually at a hotel, more rarely at their place, but never at mine, at ours. Sometimes they ask about Klaus. If they do, generally after we first have sex, I cut the affair short.

Klaus and I were one, I'd say if I were minded to explain. I lived for him and his work lived because of me. My love blazed in his work. In my heart I live for him still.

Will's unauthorised biography will soon be out. His publisher has taken out half-page ads in the literary review pages. The cover shows Klaus's face in profile. The outline of his face is a grey-brown collage of stone shapes and birds.

My memoir remains unfinished. I don't know that it will ever be written. I keep working at the opening scenes, the lavender fields of Arles, how in love we were. I write that Klaus wrote all day and devoured me at night. I write how I watched him from the bed, how I let my love burn in my eyes, how he smiled at me over his shoulder. I write that he could create only in so far as I looked upon him, heating the stone of his prose with my fire. I add that I thrived only in so far as he gazed back at me, my fire from his flint. What third party could survive within the blaze of our love?

I am pleased with this writing. It is charged and faintly titillating. Eventually, I will submit the piece to a journal somewhere as a piece of creative non-fiction, perhaps in America. Klaus is barely read in America. I want the world to know what it is to be a lifelong muse, to set fire to a genius. I want to say that it means lying within the embrace of the dead. It is a long, cold life.

Acknowledgements

Thanks so much to: Michelle Cahill, Carrol Clarkson, John Coetzee, Kwame Dawes, Gail Jones, Steven Matthews, Carol May, Tamson Pietsch, Bernard O'Donoghue, Cristóbal Perez Barra, Louis Rogers, Graham Riach, Meg Samuelson, Karina Szczurek, Terri-ann White, and everyone at Myriad Editions and the New Internationalist, especially Chris Brazier and Candida Lacey.

About the author

Elleke Boehmer was born in Durban and lives in Oxford. She is the author of five novels including *Screens Against the Sky* (shortlisted for the David Higham Prize), *Bloodlines* (shortlisted for the Sanlam Prize), *Nile Baby*, and *The Shouting in the Dark* (longlisted for the Barry Ronge *Sunday Times* prize).

She is Professor of World Literature in English at the University of Oxford. Her edition of Baden-Powell's *Scouting for Boys* was a bestseller, and her acclaimed biography of Nelson Mandela has been widely translated. Her other books include *Stories of Women*, the anthology *Empire Writing*, *Postcolonial Poetics*, and *Indian Arrivals 1870-1915: Networks of British Empire* which won the biennial ESSE 2015-16 Prize. She is a Fellow of the Royal Society of Literature.

To the Volcano, and other stories is her second collection of short stories, following *Sharmilla, and other portraits*.